"REMEMBER THAT NIGHT AT THE CASINO, WHEN I tucked your legs between mine?" Biff asked, his voice a murmur that stroked her senses into a swirl of heat and wanting.

"I remember." Her fingers tightened around the fragile wineglass as she found herself a prisoner of the excitement he created with only a suggestion. She watched, heart pounding, as he set his glass on the bar. His hands went to her legs, pushing her knees together, bracketing her with his thighs. Then, slowly, carefully, he pushed her skirt up her thighs. Her breath was coming in small gasps, the callused warmth of his hands a seductive pull she couldn't resist.

"It was about there," he said. "The dress you had on that night came up that far when you sat down. I remember being half afraid it would hitch up another inch and I'd see the tops of your stockings."

"How did you know I wore stockings?" she asked softly.

Desire sizzled in his gaze. "I knew."

WHAT ARE *LOVESWEPT* ROMANCES?

They are stories of true romance and touching emotion. We believe those two very important ingredients are constants in our highly sensual and very believable stories in the LOVESWEPT line. Our goal is to give you, the reader, stories of consistently high quality that may sometimes make you laugh, sometimes make you cry, but are always fresh and creative and contain many delightful surprises within their pages.

Most romance fans read an enormous number of books. Those they truly love, they keep. Others may be traded with friends and soon forgotten. We hope that each LOVESWEPT romance will be a treasure—a "keeper." We will always try to publish

LOVE STORIES YOU'LL NEVER FORGET
BY AUTHORS YOU'LL ALWAYS REMEMBER

The Editors

Loveswept® 646

TAKE A CHANCE ON LOVE

VICTORIA LEIGH

BANTAM BOOKS

NEW YORK · TORONTO · LONDON · SYDNEY · AUCKLAND

TAKE A CHANCE ON LOVE
A Bantam Book / October 1993

*If you would be interested in receiving protective vinyl covers for your
Loveswept books, please write to this address for information:*

> Loveswept
> Bantam Books
> P.O. Box 985
> Hicksville, NY 11802

ISBN 0-553-44229-5

Published simultaneously in the United States and Canada

PRINTED IN THE UNITED STATES OF AMERICA

OPM   0 9 8 7 6 5 4 3 2 1

TAKE A CHANCE ON LOVE

ONE

Biff tugged at the bow tie at his throat until the knot gave and the tie slipped from the starched white collar. Stomping the snow from his shoes, he tucked the length of black silk into a pocket of his black dinner jacket, then pushed through the double set of doors that were meant to keep the frigid air outside. He never should have left the hotel without a coat, he realized as an involuntary shiver overtook him, but it had seemed ridiculous to return for one after chasing the newlyweds' truck from the parking lot with a barrage of snowballs.

A blast of heat and noise engulfed him the instant the last door closed behind him. He slipped open the top buttons on his dress shirt and melted into the crowd.

The casino vibrated with a chronic energy that was an uneven mixture of triumph and defeat. Biff watched with mild curiosity as otherwise normal, rational people gambled against the odds in a frantic search for the illusive promise of a better deal. Those who had already lost their fortunes or paychecks looked on in unmasked envy as the current winners pushed their luck beyond the edge of reason.

Lady Luck was, at best, an inconsistent partner.

Biff was fully aware of a particularly juicy rumor making the rounds of local hotels and casinos regarding his own luck with gambling. According to the rumor, he'd lost a sizable fortune just last year at Hialeah Race Track in Florida. The fortune had comprised most of that year's allotment from the trust fund left him by his grandfather. The horse, a product of impeccable breeding and first-class training, had finished fifth, leaving him just enough cash in his wallet to get as far as his cousin's resort hotel on the Nevada side of Lake Tahoe. He'd been there ever since, working as a bartender in the hotel's lounge for the cousin he'd met only once before in his life.

The rumor about the horse wasn't altogether true. Biff should know. He'd started it.

For one thing he hadn't touched his trust fund in over ten years. He hadn't needed to. The income from his "real" job was more than adequate for his needs. And as for the supposed fortune he'd lost . . . Well, it hadn't been all that much.

He grinned, totally unrepentant. The bartending job suited his purposes at the moment. No one would ever imagine that the man behind the Lake Tahoe bar was a journalist whose articles graced the pages of several of the nation's most respected magazines.

Anonymity, Biff had discovered early on in his career, was at times more valuable that a fistful of high-placed sources. He'd started the rumor as a smokescreen to keep his cousin, Will Jackson, from prying into his reasons for needing a job.

Will had recently tumbled to the lie behind the rumor, but they were friends now, and Biff didn't mind sharing the truth of his real job with friends.

Looking away from the frenetic activity surrounding the craps table, he wandered deeper into the casino. A swell of sound at a nearby blackjack table caught his attention. His gaze roamed the handful of players, then sharpened on one. He felt a familiar tightening of senses—a sensation not unlike what happened when he stumbled across an especially intriguing story. His interest was firmly captured.

She was exquisite.

Partially obscured as she was by the table, spectators, and other players, Biff still managed to make a practiced assessment of her physical characteristics. Her complexion was flawless, her mouth full and luscious, her eyes wide-set and dark and heavily fringed by thick lashes. Elegant gold earrings framed her face without drawing attention away from her delicate beauty. She wore her thick rich-brown hair in a sophisticated upsweep, baring her throat and shoulders, the creamy golden flesh disappearing beneath a gown that was off-the-shoulder and totally out of this world. Biff felt his heart thump an uneven rhythm as his gaze rested upon the gentle swell of her breasts. He wondered if she wore anything of consequence beneath the gown, and hoped she didn't.

He was intensely interested in finding out.

The width of the blackjack table interrupted any perusal of her lower attributes, but one part of his mind pursued the imaginary line of hips and thighs even as his gaze followed the controlled movements of her long, supple fingers. Bare of rings, they were delicately firm as they tapped a signal to the dealer. Another card was dealt.

She won. It wasn't the first time, and the thing that had initially caught his attention happened again.

The woman didn't speak, not even to exclaim at her good fortune. Her slender fingers didn't fondle the growing pile of chips that found their way to her corner of the table. Instead she clasped her hands together, resting them on the table with almost proper precision. She was totally impassive about her win.

Not even her eyes reflected her success. Dark wells of mystery, they successfully cloaked any emotion she was experiencing. It wasn't the controlled expression of a gambler who knew the game and played the odds for a living, Biff knew. Her expression was that of total indifference, as if she wasn't even aware of what she was doing. If it hadn't been for her occasional silent instructions to the dealer, Biff would have been convinced that she was completely oblivious of her surroundings.

He was struck with the surprisingly vivid impression that she wanted to lose.

The cards were dealt. He watched as she once again bet against the odds, asking for a card when she should have stayed pat. She won.

Suddenly she lifted her gaze from the table, and Biff found himself the subject of her dark, fathomless stare. Her eyes pierced him with a fierce intensity, seeking his inner self and traveling beyond, burning him with the knowledge that her touch would be hot and exciting. He knew she wasn't merely looking through him because he could feel the living weight of her gaze upon him as if she were truly reaching out to him—needing, *wanting*! He caught his breath as fiercely erotic images crowded into his mind.

She was more exciting than any story he'd ever

written . . . more dangerous than any risk he'd undertaken in the name of research.

He didn't care.

Just as he was about to move toward her, she knit her eyebrows as if trying to recollect a past acquaintance, then shook her head when apparently nothing came to mind. Without even a smile she dropped her lashes and returned her attention to the game.

He was dismissed.

Biff forced himself to stand there, watching . . . daring her to do it again. The minutes passed, and eventually he steeled himself to accept her disregard. It wasn't so much that his body cooled and his desire waned. Rather he shook off the absolute surprise of her fiery attack and plotted his own strike.

Her pile of winnings grew higher. He watched her defy the odds time and time again, his gaze occasionally sweeping the crowd for signs of a companion. She was alone, he finally decided. For the moment anyway. None of the men at or around the table was giving out proprietary signals.

She won again, and this time Biff knew he was right. Her grimace of distaste was unmistakable.

The crowd cooed their appreciation as the dealer slid several stacks of chips across the green baize table. Several thousand dollars' worth of chips sat in front of the dark-haired beauty, a considerable increase from the smaller stack he'd noticed when he first started watching. Biff was calculating the odds against her winning yet again, when she slipped off her chair and walked swiftly away from the table.

She left behind the entire pile of chips.

Biff was already on the move when he noticed the

dealer signal the pit boss. They'd catch up with her. He intended to get there first.

He didn't have to move very fast to keep her in sight. The crowds were thick at this end of the casino, shifting currents of bodies straining to see or play or just get out into the fresh air. He followed in her wake as she strolled through the maze of excited gamblers and gawking tourists. She wasn't in a hurry anymore, he realized. It seemed as though the more distance she put between herself and the blackjack table, the slower she walked.

He trailed her across the casino floor and into an adjoining passage. Ducking through the curtained doorway, Biff found himself in a quietly elegant cocktail lounge, far removed from the clanging bells and half-demented shouts of the room outside. He blinked slowly, forcing his eyes to adjust to the reduced lighting.

When he looked again, he caught sight of her climbing onto a stool at the far end of the bar. Sensing movement behind him, he turned to find a casino employee lifting a walkie-talkie to his mouth. The woman had been found and cornered. Biff knew the powers-that-be would soon descend with the chips she'd left behind. It simply wasn't done to walk away from one's winnings. Taking advantage of the momentary lull in activity, he crossed the room. His first glimpse of her long, shapely legs prompted a surge of warmth through his body. He smiled his pleasure at his physical response and slid onto an adjoining stool just in time to hear her order a bottle of champagne.

For someone who had been so annoyed at winning, he thought, she was taking it rather well.

"How much is it?" she asked, her voice a husky rub on his senses as she opened the purse in her lap.

"Anywhere from twenty to two hundred dollars," the bartender said. "Your choice."

Her eyes widened, and she took a deep breath before slipping her fingers into her purse. Clearly she hadn't realized champagne could be so expensive.

Biff was more than a little surprised when she pulled out two one-hundred-dollar bills and laid them on the bar. Looking neither right nor left, she snapped her purse shut and flipped it onto the bar, acting for all the world as though she didn't realize there was another person seated next to her. The lounge was nearly empty, and it had to be obvious he'd taken that stool out of choice and not necessity.

"We have several different . . ." the bartender began.

Biff took his cue. "Taittinger."

He watched closely as she reacted to him—her back stiffening in surprise, her fingers finding the edge of the bar in a tense clutch. A moment, that was all she took to find her nerve.

When she turned to face him, her expression was curiously blank. Her body language had been full of tension, yet now there was no hint of it.

He admired her reflexes. She had to know he'd followed her from the casino, but she didn't show it. She just stared at him and waited.

"The Taittinger should pretty much take care of that," he said, nodding toward the pair of bills on the bar.

She glanced aside, first at the money and then at the bartender, appearing surprised to find he was still hovering. She gave him a quick nod and turned back to Biff.

She didn't speak, not right away. He watched her expression as she studied him. He was a long way from handsome, he knew, although experience had taught him that the lean, almost harsh lines of his face were attractive to some. His straight hair brushed the collar of his shirt and was nearly the same dark brown as his eyes.

There wasn't even a hint of recognition as her gaze traveled over his face, sharpening momentarily on the narrow, inch-long scar that ran vertically along the outside edge of his cheek just below his eye. It intrigued him when she didn't say anything about it.

Some women were repelled by it, just as others were fascinated. Biff had long ago learned to live with their questions, revulsions, and even the odd romantic fantasy about how he'd come by it.

He'd never met a woman who didn't seem to care one way or the other. He was pleased.

Her gaze lifted to meet his, her eyes deep pools of brown that invited without being inviting. He wondered how she did that. It was as if she wanted him to stay but knew better.

"If you were a wise man, you'd run for the hills," she said finally, her words laced with the skeptical mistrust a woman was supposed to feel in this kind of situation. They were, after all, complete strangers.

"Now, why on earth should I do that?" He leaned an elbow on the bar and turned his body more fully toward her. Not aggressively, but deliberately. He was telling her that he intended to stay, wise decision or not.

Her gaze swept him from head to toe as she measured his determination. A reluctant smile hinted at her lips. "To be perfectly honest, I'm in a foul mood and you look much too dangerous a man to annoy with it."

"I don't annoy easily."

"That doesn't make you any less dangerous," she said

softly, her eyes darkening with recognition of that danger.

"I'll take my chances."

"What if I told you I'm on my honeymoon?"

It shook him, her quiet words sweeping aside like so much rubbish the excitement he'd imagined sharing with her. His disappointment was so intense, he couldn't be bothered to try to hide it. He stared at her and wondered why her husband had left her to wander the casino alone. Obviously their marriage wasn't off to a great start.

He dropped his gaze to her hands, avoiding her stare because those beautiful eyes were such a temptation. He knew he had to leave before he made an ass out of himself.

There were no rings on her fingers.

His head jerked up, and he pinned her with his stare. "You're not married."

"I came close," she said, "but close only counts in horseshoes and hand grenades."

"Your honeymoon," he said gently. "Not turning out exactly as you hoped?"

She shook her head, smiling wryly.

"Are you angry because the marriage didn't happen?"

"Only that I even considered it. I was an idiot to imagine that Anthony was in love with me. I got exactly what I deserved."

"Anthony's a fool," he said succinctly, liking the sound of it.

"Now you see why I'm not the best of company. It doesn't sit well that I allowed myself to be . . . manipulated."

There was more here than a broken engagement. Biff tucked that bit of information aside for later study and said, "I'm still willing to take my chances."

She looked as though she couldn't decide whether to

be piqued by his persistence or interested by his attention. For all that Biff could tell from her expression of aloof detachment, it ended in a draw.

But she didn't leave.

Nor did she give him the slightest bit of encouragement. She just sat with one hand on the edge of the bar, the other in her lap and her gaze trained on him.

Waiting.

"I followed you from the casino."

"I know," she said immediately, but didn't by so much as a glance let him know if she cared one way or the other.

He needed her to admit that she cared, that that look she'd leveled on him in the casino hadn't been one hundred percent his imagination.

"Tell me something?" he said.

"What?"

"Back in the casino, when you looked at me."

She smiled immediately, a mischievous look that diminished her air of sophisticated reserve and supplanted it with a playfulness that he found incredibly provocative.

"What about it?" she asked, all coolness gone as she almost seemed to dare him to proceed.

"What were you looking for?"

"What makes you think I was looking for anything?"

He shook his head, then waited until her pretty smile faded and she was as serious as he. "What were you thinking?" he asked.

"I don't know," she said, her voice a thready whisper. "It isn't something I can really explain. I just looked up because I knew you were there."

"You knew before you looked?"

She nodded. "And I felt . . ." Her words trailed off, her eyes clouding with confusion.

"You felt what?" he pressed, leaning toward her so that he wouldn't miss anything. "What did you feel?"

She stared at him in bewilderment. "I think . . . I felt the same thing you did."

Biff smiled and knew that his instincts hadn't been wrong. There was something extraordinarily special about this woman that tugged at his senses with a power he'd never felt before.

The fact that she'd practically admitted to feeling the same thing was a satisfying bonus.

The bartender returned with the champagne and two tulip-shaped glasses. The woman gave the label a dutiful glance, then again sought Biff's gaze as the bottle was opened and poured.

"Last chance," she said, and bit down on her lip, her hesitation slowing the invitation that was plain in her eyes. "I'm really not very good company tonight."

He reached for the two glasses. Her hand was trembling as he gave her one, the white heat of awareness sparking between them as they touched . . . her fingers drifting across his, then sliding down to take the stemmed crystal from him.

Their eyes met in a silent toast, then he tasted the cold, bubbling wine on his lips. Taittinger was a treat he hadn't allowed himself recently.

"Does it frighten you?" he asked, cutting corners that he probably shouldn't cut, but what the hell. He could no more control the pace than he could walk away from her.

"Does what frighten me?"

"Knowing that something is happening to us."

"*To* us?" Her eyebrows lifted in amused skepticism. The playfulness was back.

"To us."

She studied him for a moment, then shook her head. "Slick words," she said. "Certainly a more interesting approach than saying that something might happen *between* us."

"There's that, too," he agreed, "but it's not everything."

"A proposition with depth," she countered, and looked as if she was actually enjoying their little game of words. "How unique."

A frown creased his forehead. "Unique, yes. But a proposition?" He shook his head. "It's not that simple."

"Okay, I'll bite." She took a small sip from her glass. "Just what is this thing that might happen to us?"

"Not *might* happen. *Is* happening." His gaze softened as it wandered over her creamy shoulders and the swell of her breasts. She was so incredibly exotic-looking, her figure showcased by a dynamite black dress, the enticing mass of her hair, and her flawless skin. It was a temptation that he was finding increasingly difficult to resist. His fingers flexed as he felt the excitement build, and his gaze returned to hers.

"I can't explain any more because I really don't know," he said.

"How do you know I'm even interested?"

He grinned. "Because you're still here."

"Aren't you concerned that I might be on the rebound?"

"You're angry, not brokenhearted," he said firmly. "And you're as attracted to me as I am to you. That's not something you can turn your back on, not when it's this strong."

She blushed, her cheeks brightening with the heat of her unconscious reaction.

He chuckled, a gently chiding laugh that expressed his pleasure at her response. He touched her there, on the soft skin of her cheek, his thumb stroking the awareness she couldn't hide. She shivered, but didn't retreat.

Biff made his hand fall away when the tip of her tongue slipped out to wet her lips. He wanted so very badly to open his mouth on hers, to show her another way to bring moisture there.

He knew better than to carry through with his thoughts, not with that vaguely wary look still in her eyes. She didn't quite trust him.

In the next moment, though, she lifted her own hand to her cheek, her expression confused as she touched the same place his thumb had caressed. For a moment, no more, then the look of mistrust was back.

She didn't *want* to trust him.

Listen to your instincts, he longed to tell her. *Trust me*. But he didn't say anything because it was something she would have to discover for herself. He wouldn't hurt her, not ever.

She needed time. He was going to give it to her.

Out of the corner of his eye he noticed the man with the walkie-talkie had been joined by another man, and they were headed their way.

"Have you given any thought to what you're going to do about that pile of chips you left back on the table?" he asked. She shrugged and took another sip of champagne, obviously not intending to do anything at all.

"Miss?" Visibly startled, she looked at the men and glanced back at Biff as understanding dawned. Sighing, she turned to the duo and said, "Is there something I can do for you, gentlemen?"

"There's a small matter of your winnings that you left at the blackjack table," the older one said.

"So?"

"So . . . no one just walks away from thousands of dollars," he said, dragging a pudgy finger between his neck and shirt collar. The other one, much younger but just as uncomfortable-looking, was staring at her as though she'd recently grown a second head.

"I did," she said.

"But why?"

"I left it because I didn't want it," she said, carefully enunciating each word. "Surely that much is obvious?"

"We don't have a policy covering that," the older man said. Before she could protest, he pulled a wad of bills from inside his jacket and put it on the bar beside her. "I cashed them in for you. Four thousand five hundred and eighty-five dollars."

"I don't want it."

"You can tip the dealer if you wish—"

"I don't want it."

"There are some expensive shops in the lobby where you can spend it all in just a few minutes," he continued as though she hadn't spoken.

"I don't want it."

"Or you can try to lose it at the tables."

"I don't want it."

"Enjoy your stay," he said, and turned on his heel before she could say it again.

The other one hesitated for a moment, as though he was going to advise her on the most expedient way to get rid of four-thousand-plus dollars, but apparently decided it wasn't in his job description. Wishing her luck, he followed the other man out of the lounge.

"This is ridiculous," she muttered, eyeing the small stack of mostly large-denomination bills with a baleful stare. "Where's a pickpocket when you need one?"

Biff studied her for a moment, then poured more champagne into her glass. Why should he care if she wanted to throw her money away? If she could pop for two-hundred-dollar champagne, he assumed she could afford it.

Still, he couldn't help but be curious. "Why *did* you walk away from your winnings?"

She grimaced, then sneezed as a couple of bubbles snuck into her nose. "I was trying to lose."

"That part was obvious. That's one of the reasons I was watching you. You seemed annoyed that you were winning." She looked surprised, and he shrugged. "It's no fun to watch someone lose, but a disgruntled winner . . . now, that's an event."

She toyed with her glass, twirling the fragile stem between her fingers. "I've played blackjack before and never had this problem." She sighed, and stared at the glass as though the solution might be somewhere within.

"I still don't think I understand," he said. "Why play if you don't want to win?"

She had the grace to look faintly embarrassed. "Would you believe I just wanted to go back home with my pockets empty?"

"Why not simply spend it like the man suggested?"

"Because then I'll have something to take home to remind me of this weekend," she said softly.

So that was it.

Biff took a deep breath and followed the thread of logic. "Your honeymoon money."

She nodded. "I saved it especially for this weekend, and damned if I'm not going to get rid of every cent."

"A catharsis."

She nodded again.

Biff watched over the crystal rim of his glass as she swallowed some champagne, then sipped again, her gaze never once leaving his. She still halfway clutched the bar with one hand, steadying herself with her knees toward the bar and her face toward him. It had to be awkward, he realized. Perhaps it was just her way of maintaining her distance.

He decided he didn't like it.

"You're going to get a crick in your neck," he said, setting his glass on the bar. Her gaze followed his down to where his own legs straddled the backless stool, heels caught on the lower rung, facing her.

She actually grinned. "I don't think I can do that."

He stared at the tightly fitting black velvet sheath that ended several inches above her knees and nodded. "I didn't imagine that you could." In the next second his hands were at her waist and he was turning her on the stool so that her knees were bracketed between his legs.

He heard her swift intake of breath and suddenly questioned the wisdom of what he'd just done. The slightest shift in either direction would bring her knees against his thighs.

"Better?" he asked, his voice rough with the anticipation of what might happen.

She took another sip of champagne and nodded. There was a momentary distraction as an exuberant group crowded through the door. The noise level increased as they shifted several nearby tables and chairs until there was an irregular circle big enough to accommodate all of them. Biff watched as the woman beside him eyed the crowd with clear misgivings. He agreed with her. The near-privacy of the lounge had been violated.

He wondered if she'd go with him for dinner. Somewhere quietly romantic, but first things first.

"Don't you think it's time we introduced ourselves?" he asked when her gaze finally left the newcomers.

"Is it absolutely necessary?"

He waggled his eyebrows and grinned. "I don't make a habit of being this intimate with total strangers."

"Intimate?"

"Almost to the point of being . . . engaged, one might say."

She followed his glance downward and blushed. Then, with a show of bravado that he imagined was as much the influence of the champagne as it was genuine defiance, she looked him straight in the eye and said, "Smile when you say that word, buster."

He smiled.

She smiled back and said, "I'm Amanda Lawrence."

"Barley Fuller," he said with a slight bow. "At your service."

"Barley?" she repeated, an incredulous note in her voice.

"It's an old family name," he said, grinning. "You can call me by my nickname, if you like."

"And that is . . . ?"

"Biff."

She looked as though she was going to choke over a giggle. He had to give her credit when she managed to muffle it.

"Biff Fuller," she finally said aloud. She looked as though she was considering an appropriate comment, when her knees moved a critical two inches.

He discovered what it was like to feel as though he'd been struck by lightning. His breath caught in his throat, and he knew there was a certain wildness in his gaze when he forced his eyes to meet hers.

She'd felt it too. He knew that, because her smile was gone, replaced by an expression of arousal mingled with astonishment. He watched, fascinated, as her breaths came shallow and quick. When she began to ease her knee away from his thigh, he stopped her with the firm touch of his hand.

"Don't move," he said huskily. "Not unless you're afraid."

Shaking her head, she whispered, "I'm not afraid."

He didn't believe her, but he let her get away with it because his own nerves were on the jumpy side. He had to give her credit, though. Even though the wary look had returned to cloud her eyes, she didn't move—at least not until a few moments later, when she excused herself to go to the rest room.

She never came back. But then, he hadn't really expected her to.

Biff waited thirty minutes, then stood and shoved the four and a half thousand dollars into his pocket, leaving the eighty-five for the bartender. A month, he decided as he walked slowly through the casino toward the outside door.

It should be enough time for her. Bruised pride and wounded feelings would have begun to heal. She would be more centered when he saw her again, more trusting of her instincts.

More trusting of him.

Biff knew he'd need every bit of that month to get his own life in order. Besides the practical details that went with quitting his extra job and moving, there was the matter of the story he'd recently committed to writing on modern-day gold mining in the Sierras. While the dead-line was several months down the road, it made sense to get it out of the way so that he could concentrate on Amanda.

In the meantime all he had to do was find her . . . and try to discover what it was besides a broken engagement that troubled her.

For all the good it did, Biff pulled up the collar of his dinner jacket and let himself outside to where the temperatures were plunging to record depths. He bent into the wind and slowly made his way along the salt-roughened sidewalk toward the hotel.

A month, he told himself, wasn't an eternity.

It would just feel like it.

TWO

Amanda slammed the door to her second-story condominium and skipped down the wooden staircase to the carport below. Sliding behind the wheel of her 1958 Hillman Husky, she pumped the gas pedal and prayed for a miracle.

The cute little red car with beige side panels never failed to let her down when she needed it most, which was why she knew every taxi driver in the town of Larkspur, California, by name, first *and* last.

Today she simply wasn't in the mood for idle chatter.

The car coughed, sputtered, and died. She tried it again, not losing heart because the first round always went that way, regardless of the eventual outcome. Another cough, a sputter, and the ancient engine did a credible imitation of roaring to life, the roar being more of a gentle giggle and the life it aspired to a very tenuous grasp on reality indeed.

Amanda didn't waste time heaving deep breaths of

gratitude, but threw the Husky into gear and worked her way out of the parking lot. Two minutes later, car and driver were humming along the Redwood Highway toward San Rafael, where Amanda had a meeting with her attorney.

Blayne Martin, the husband of one of her best friends from college, was a highly respected member of the Bay Area's legal community. He'd been advising Amanda almost from the beginning, when Mandy's Candies had been a two-person operation working out of her own kitchen. Now, with over thirty employees and a reputation that extended all the way to the East Coast, Mandy's Candies was one of his most visible clients.

More accurately Mandy's Candies *had* been one of his most visible clients.

Too bad she'd mucked it up, Amanda thought, pulling in behind a semi that was exceeding the speed limit by a satisfactory margin. Not that there was anything the matter with the relationship between Mandy's Candies and their legal adviser. No, it was much worse than that.

Amanda, as sole owner and manager of the highly successful candy emporium, which offered petits fours and similarly exquisite delicacies, had decided to merge with a large and so-called reputable gourmet food company. Expansion had always been her dream. Classic Foods had made a proposal that made that very expansion possible. With Amanda at the helm to maintain control of the quality and standards for which Mandy's Candies was famous, they proposed to open shops in several major cities.

They hadn't lied. A month ago she'd signed the merger contract, and already plans were being made for the expansion. That was the upside. The downside was that Classic Foods had exercised their option of choosing their own management team.

Amanda wasn't on it. In fact she didn't have anything at all to do with Mandy's Candies.

They'd fired her a month ago.

Amanda had asked her attorney to do what he had to do to get her company back. It hadn't looked good, but she had complete faith in Blayne. She still did, even though his periodic reports had been disappointingly full of his lack of progress and not the other way around.

She refused to believe he couldn't get her out of this mess. That this mess was of her own making was as embarrassing as it was aggravating. She'd ignored Blayne's best advice and her own misgivings and had thus ended up making the worst decision of her life.

But then, the decision to run away from the mysterious, kind, *exciting* man she'd met in Tahoe had been no less reckless. She wished now that she could go back and do it again . . . stay with him, be with him. Life didn't give second chances, though.

Biff. She smiled, her usual reaction when she thought of him by that name. Barley was better, and she found herself liking it more than Biff.

Still, Biff wasn't so bad once she'd gotten used to it.

Biff or Barley, Amanda thought of him often, wishing she'd made a different decision . . . and knowing there hadn't been another one to make. She'd been too raw that night, hurting as only a woman used could hurt. She hadn't trusted herself to be with him, or with any man for that matter.

In the four weeks since she'd hightailed it out of Tahoe, she'd had plenty of time to regret her cowardice. The decision to leave had been reflex, Anthony's fault really, but still something for which she could blame no one but herself.

Another bad decision, Amanda had realized before she'd even reached the foothills of the western slopes beneath the pass at Echo Summit.

It worried her that she might be on a roll.

She'd reached her exit, and she pulled to the right, slipping into the exit lane and cutting her speed to something appropriate for city streets. Blayne's office was easily reached—that is, if one knew which way the one-way streets ran and which private parking lots turned a blind eye to vintage automobiles. Pulling into the lot by Blayne's building, Amanda turned off the ignition with trepidation, knowing that the next time she got into the car, it might very well play dead.

It didn't matter, though. She'd happily cab it for the next year once Blayne explained how he was going to save her butt from permanent retirement.

She didn't even know what Barley Fuller did for a living, she realized.

She'd probably never know.

With a sigh and an effort at a smile that was for the sole benefit of the parking attendant, Amanda slid out of the antique Hillman and walked briskly toward the cluster of red-clay buildings that housed Blayne and his partners.

She couldn't wait to hear what he'd come up with.

"There's got to be something you haven't tried." Amanda stared mutinously at the dark-haired man sitting behind the polished mahogany desk. "I don't intend to just roll over and let Anthony take Mandy's Candies without a fight."

"Read my lips, Amanda," Blayne said with no hint of humor. "I told you before you went to Tahoe that things weren't looking too good. Since then I've gone over the contract more than a dozen times, and nothing has changed. There are no loopholes. You have no company, no job—"

"There's *got* to be something we can do," she interrupted, frustration welling up in her to the point where she was ready to scream.

"Not legally."

"But Mandy's Candies is my baby," she whispered, anguish filling her to near overflowing.

"Was," Blayne said firmly. "Give it up, Amanda. It's over."

She muttered something under her breath that reeked of her contrary intentions.

Blayne sighed heavily. "Didn't anyone ever tell you it's a waste of money to keep an attorney on retainer if you don't take his advice?"

Amanda grimaced and squirmed in the leather chair. "I knew you'd get around to that eventually."

"To what?" He raised his eyebrows questioningly.

"To telling me 'I told you so' of course. Ever since this whole mess started, I know you've been dying to say it."

Blayne twirled the tip of his letter opener on the pad of his middle finger and shook his head in gentle reproof. "This isn't a joke, Amanda. If you'd listened to me in the first place, you wouldn't be in this position."

"Hell, Blayne, I didn't even listen to *myself*! I *knew* better than to sign that contract!"

His normally harsh features softened, and she remembered what a caring friend he'd been to her.

"You were in love—" he began.

"I was infatuated," she corrected him quickly. "If I'd been in love, I'd be too heartbroken now to worry about what Anthony stole from me." *You're angry, not brokenhearted . . . you're as attracted to me as I am to you. That's not something you can turn your back on, not when it's this strong.*

Biff's words came back to her loud and clear. He was right in more ways than she'd been able to admit that night in Tahoe.

He was also a risk, one she hadn't been ready for so soon after Anthony's betrayal. She'd known that, given a chance, Biff might have someday broken her heart. Not intentionally, but because that was what happened when things fell apart between two people . . . two people who had shared tenderness, affection, and intimacies.

But he wouldn't have cheated her. She believed that, yet couldn't help but fear that she was, once again, leading with her heart instead of her head. She took a deep breath and wondered how long it would be before she could dare trust herself again.

Even when she *knew* she was right.

She hoped.

Holding Blayne's gaze, she restated the obvious. "As I said, Blayne, I wasn't really in love. Anthony took advantage of my infatuation to steal Mandy's Candies from me."

"Technically that's a slanderous statement," Blayne said. "Try to remember not to repeat it outside these walls, hmm?" There was a soft buzz, and he leaned forward to pick up the telephone.

Amanda waited with barely concealed impatience as Blayne listened, taking a sip from her coffee cup before setting it back on the desk. She wasn't going to let him give up, not if she had to spend all day convincing him of it. Her thoughts were interrupted when his gaze suddenly narrowed on her, his brows arching in apparent surprise. She gave him a sassy look in return, followed by an annoyed one when he said, "Send him in, Margie," and put down the phone.

"Send who in?" she demanded.

The look he gave her was curiously enigmatic. "You tell me."

She twisted awkwardly in her chair to watch as the door opened behind her. Blayne's secretary came in and stepped aside, allowing the man with her to enter. She left, pulling the door closed with a click.

Her first thought was that she must be hallucinating. She blinked once, then again, but the apparition didn't vanish. She stared harder, taking note of how good he looked in jeans as he hesitated just inside the door. His fawn-colored sport coat was unbuttoned, his tie loose around the collar of his shirt, where he'd unfastened the top button. With his hands shoved into his back pockets, the shirt was stretched taut across his chest.

When her gaze reached his face, it was to discover that the image she'd carried of him in her mind for the past month had been extraordinarily accurate. Dark-brown eyes twinkled out at her from beneath his brows, the tiny scar just visible from where she was sitting, his firm mouth curved as if he were on the edge of laughter. Details filled her mind, pushing aside for the moment such practical questions as how he came to be there, why, and . . . Well, just how and why.

Or if. She wasn't even certain of that much. Nothing like wishful thinking for producing hallucinations.

"Sorry to barge in like this, Amanda. I thought it

would save time, though. It's not like you have a lot to spare."

The figment of her imagination even got the voice right, although what he was saying was pure gibberish. She opened her mouth to say something along those lines, but caught herself in the nick of time.

One didn't speak to an hallucination. Turning to face Blayne, she smiled weakly and wondered how she was going to explain her temporary inattention. But Blayne was standing up behind his desk, his attention fixed on a point behind her.

She slipped another look over her shoulder and saw that it was still there. Him. Barley Fuller. Biff. In the flesh.

"Amanda?" Blayne's voice cut across her stunned acknowledgment.

"Hmm?"

She continued staring at Barley. The reality of his presence sent a shiver of excitement zinging through her already tingling nerves.

Why was he there?

"Why?" Her voice was a gravelly whisper that nevertheless managed to reach Biff. He pulled his hands out of his pockets and crossed to her.

"Because you need help." He touched her lightly on the shoulder, then turned to Blayne and held out his hand. "I'm Biff Fuller, a friend of Amanda's. Kind of."

Blayne introduced himself and shook the offered hand. The single brow inching up his forehead was his only sign of curiosity. "Kind of?"

"A recent friend. We met last month in Tahoe." Biff took a piece of paper from his pocket and handed it to Blayne.

Blayne's glance flicked over the paper. "Impressive," he said after a moment, studying Biff with more interest before returning his gaze to the paper.

Disgruntled at being ignored, Amanda asked, "What is it, Blayne?"

"Mostly it's a list of people who live in the area. There is one name I don't recognize, though."

Amanda tugged at Biff's jacket to get his attention. "What's this all about?"

His smile was gentle as he hunkered down to come to eye level with her. "You need help, Amanda. I'd like to take a shot at helping you save Mandy's Candies."

Her gaze narrowed suspiciously. "How did you know? I didn't say anything in Tahoe." She'd made it a point to keep the whole humiliating story to herself, a matter of pride and all that.

"You didn't have to say anything. It was simple to see that your unhappiness extended way beyond a broken engagement."

"That doesn't explain how you found out," she declared mutinously. Shades of Anthony, she mused, comparing Biff's surprising knowledge of her business affairs with Anthony's underhanded manipulation of the same.

She hated comparing him with Anthony.

"I'll explain all that later," he said without expression. "For now all you need to believe is that I want to help you."

"What makes you think I can trust you any further than I can trust the man who stole Mandy's Candies from me?"

His eyes went dark with anger, and she realized she'd just insulted him. Before she could apologize, though, his expression cleared and he took a deep breath. "I don't blame you for not trusting me, Amanda. In fact that's why I brought the list." He indicated the paper Blayne was studying. "Those are references, I guess you'd say. The first name is my cousin, Will Jackson. He'll vouch for my general trustworthiness."

"And the others?" This from Blayne.

"Friends and/or business acquaintances of my cousin. I couldn't be sure you'd know enough about him to trust what he said, so I brought along a list of people he knew would vouch for him, people who are generally well known and respected in this area. I was hoping we'd find common ground somewhere among them."

Blayne nodded approvingly and handed the list to Amanda, who took it without letting her gaze leave Biff's. "This is ludicrous. I hardly know you and you're trying to involve yourself in something that means my whole world to me."

He cupped her chin with his fingers. "If it wasn't so important, I wouldn't have presumed to interrupt your meeting."

"But how—" It didn't make sense, his being there, his knowing she needed him.

She needed him. Now, that made even less sense.

Biff just shook his head. "Leave the details alone for a bit. For now you need to establish that you can trust me, that I am who I say I am." He dropped his fingers from her chin and glanced at his watch. "I'll be in the lounge at the end of the hall. When you've finished checking me out, you can make a more informed decision about whether or not you think I can help, and if you want me to. I'll wait for an hour."

She swallowed and said nothing as he stood, nodded briskly at Blayne, and strode out the door.

"Well?" Blayne folded his hands on the desk and waited for Amanda's decision. "I'm not sure what that was all about, but I like his approach."

She looked at him incredulously. "He interrupted a private meeting, Blayne. Don't you think that's a bit presumptuous?"

Blayne just shrugged. "Perhaps, but he was right about one thing. Two things actually."

"What?"

"You need help—his help—and you're almost out of time."

"I thought you said nothing could be done."

"That was before I met your friend."

Amanda studied her attorney before asking, "What makes you think he can help?"

"Instinct." He grinned and held out his hand. "Now, unless you have any qualms about this, hand me that list. I should be able to get some answers that will satisfy us both."

Hell yes, she had qualms. But she handed him the list anyway, fully aware of the risk she was taking.

With her heart.

Barley was alone in the lounge. The late-morning sun threw his shadow across the floor from where he stood looking out the window. Her footsteps were silent on the thick carpet as she entered the room, but she realized that he was aware of her. Perhaps responding to a change in the air around him, perhaps just tired of looking out the window, he turned and gave her a curious look.

"Well?"

She took a deep breath and shot a nervous glance around the room. "Blayne says I can trust you."

"That's not good enough." He put down the Styrofoam cup he'd been holding and walked toward her, plucking her gaze from its wavering path and holding it with his own. "The question is whether or not you trust me."

She swallowed hard and gave herself a moment to think. Blayne had talked with several of the men on the list, one of them a close friend of his. All had given Biff's cousin their highest praise, both business and personal. Using those recommendations as a springboard, Blayne had then called Will Jackson. Without giving away many details, Jackson had done much the same for his cousin. Biff, he said, was trustworthy, honorable, and handy to have around in a crisis. What he did for a living, though, was still a mystery.

Blayne had pronounced Biff's references impeccable, if a little vague. It surprised Amanda to realize how little they still knew. But Blayne had been more than satisfied, as was she.

Instinct merged with what they'd learned in those few telephone calls. She trusted Barley. She had from the beginning, even though common sense had made her take certain precautions. Her heart had led her to make rotten decisions with Anthony.

"I trust you." She didn't define how. It would have sounded silly saying "I trust you with Mandy's Candies, but fully realize you can't be responsible if my heart decides to get involved."

He nodded as though he understood, then smiled wickedly—a smile she recognized. "What do you say we go back and get this meeting over with, darling? I'm sure

Blayne has other things on his agenda." He planted a quick kiss on the tip of her nose, then took hold of her elbow and urged her back down the hall at a brisk pace as Amanda tried to regain the breath his endearment had knocked out of her. And the kiss.

He'd kissed her! Her mind did instant replays as they walked down the hall and into the law offices. He'd kissed her! On the nose.

Not exactly the stuff of passionate romances, but a kiss all the same. She succeeded in taking a deep, calming breath . . . which didn't calm her at all.

"Darling?" she finally managed to say, her heart still thumping madly as she turned her head to stare at Biff.

His expression went all soft and sexy. "I love it when you call me that." He led her past the secretary and into the inner office where Blayne was waiting.

Her face became suffused with color, and Biff chuckled, a gentle laugh of genuine masculine appreciation of her reaction. "Remind me to tease you about that blush of yours when we get back home," he said, his words deliberately implying that they'd been there before. Together, at her home.

"What?" Amanda shook her head in an attempt to reorganize her scattered thoughts. The attempt was unsuccessful.

"When we're alone, darling," Biff said. Then he looked past her, a grin on his face as he reminded her there was a witness to the scene between them.

From behind his desk Blayne cleared his throat. "Somehow, Amanda, I was under the impression you'd only met once, in Tahoe. But then, I suppose your private life is your own." He motioned for them to sit in the chairs in front of his desk. "Still, Biff's offer to help would have made more sense if you'd told me."

"Told you what?" She stared at him in total confusion, taking her seat because her knees were surprisingly weak. Slouching in her chair, she decided the pressure had finally gotten to her.

She needed a time-out. She'd corner Biff on that "darling" act later. In private.

"Never mind," Blayne said. "We need to get on with this." Turning his head, he looked at Biff. "I take it you have a good picture of what's going on."

"Pretty much." Biff reached across the space that separated him from Amanda and stroked her forearm, a comforting gesture that just about sent her ballistic. "I know that Classic Foods offered a merger to Mandy's Candies. The agreement was signed a month ago. They sacked Amanda right after that."

Blayne said, "I've been trying to find a way to nullify the contract, but as I've just told Amanda, there's nothing we can do. Once escrow is over, Mandy's Candies will belong to Classic Foods, and Amanda is out of a job. Permanently."

"Airtight and legal?"

Blayne nodded.

"What if Classic Foods wanted out of the contract? Is that legally possible?"

"Technically yes. Escrow doesn't close for another two weeks. The bulk of the payment for Mandy's Candies is due at that time. If Parks doesn't pay in full, the business would simply revert to Amanda."

Amanda snorted. "Fat chance!" Her words borrowed the men's attention for a second before they returned to the discussion at hand. She slouched deeper in her chair and ground her teeth in frustration, time-out over.

"So how did she already get fired if the deal hasn't closed yet?" Biff asked.

"Fine print." Blayne leveled a reproving glance at Amanda. "On the surface their willingness to step in immediately and begin the expansion effort while still in escrow demonstrated an act of good faith."

"Interesting," Biff murmured.

Blayne shot Amanda a speculative look before asking Biff, "Were you aware that Anthony Parks, the managing director of Classic Foods, was Amanda's fiancé?"

Biff nodded curtly. "I'm aware of the facts."

Blayne looked as if he were going to fill him in, when Amanda surged to her feet. It rankled her that she'd been such a fool. Even worse, she hated having Biff know that she'd messed up, professionally as well as emotionally.

For some reason she wanted him to think she was a little smarter than she appeared. She began to pace, her anger replacing the bemused excitement of Biff's unexpected kiss. "That thief stole Mandy's Candies from me!" she insisted, the low heels of her pumps sinking into the plush Oriental carpet with every step. Her short wool skirt was tight enough to inhibit her taking long steps, but she still managed to cover the length of Blayne's office in half a dozen paces.

Blayne shook his head decisively. "He didn't steal it," he told Biff. "Amanda still has minority interest—"

"Which gets me nothing except a share of the profits," she huffed. "If all I'd wanted was to make money, I would have sold him the company outright."

"It's actually quite common for senior management to get sacked after a merger," Blayne said, obviously speaking for Biff's benefit because Amanda had heard this at least a dozen times. Not that she accepted it, but she'd heard it. "Parks's company has majority interest in Mandy's Candies now. He can do whatever he wants with the management thereof, which includes firing Amanda."

"That wasn't supposed to be part of the deal! I'd never have signed if I'd realized what he intended." Her words trailed off as she once again faced how Anthony had manipulated her.

"It was in the contract," Blayne said.

"I *know* it was in the contract!"

"Then why did you sign?" Biff asked quietly.

She flashed him a look of frustration. It was too late now, too late to avoid looking like the fool she'd been. She hated having to reveal the whole sordid mess to Biff.

He was waiting, though, and she realized she no longer had a choice.

"He convinced me that he believed Mandy's Candies wouldn't be the same without me. He said that without me running things, they wouldn't be interested in the merger at all." She began pacing again, throwing off the wool jacket as her body temperature responded to her heated temper. The white silk blouse that she wore beneath it hugged her figure, caressing her with every movement she made.

She scowled in the general direction of the two men without missing a step. "How was I supposed to know that, quote, 'management of Mandy's Candies will be at the sole discretion of Classic Foods,' unquote, meant that he was going to get rid of me the second I signed the contract?"

"You didn't even suspect that you'd lose control?" Biff asked, his head following her furious pacing as if he were watching a tennis match.

Amanda refused to look at him, too embarrassed to admit that she'd squelched her own misgivings with difficulty. It hadn't made good business sense to let herself be talked into signing away management of her company, but she'd thought with her heart instead of her head.

At least she was learning something. Now she was using both.

She shook her head furiously, long strands of hair coming loose from the chignon at her nape. She impatiently tucked them behind her ear, then wrapped her arms around her waist as she whirled to face the men.

"There's got to be something we can do!"

Only silence met her heated words. Silence, and the knowledge that she'd lost the one thing in her life that had been hers. Blood rushed to her face as she remembered Anthony's expression the moment she'd put down the pen after signing the merger contract. It had been victorious, and for the first time she'd noticed a hint of cunning.

Suddenly, though, it had been champagne and congratulations all around, and she'd nearly convinced herself that she'd imagined what she'd seen in his eyes. But when she'd lifted her glass to meet Anthony's in that first toast, she'd known with certainty that something was wrong, terribly wrong. In his eyes had been the satisfied expression of a predator who had bagged his quarry. Love? There hadn't been a trace of it.

She'd known then that she'd lost it all.

"You never intended to marry me, did you?"

His smile chilled her. *"I would have, but when you signed those papers, it became . . . unnecessary."*

"I thought you loved me." Staring across the table at the boyishly handsome man with whom she'd shared the ultimate in intimacies, she wondered how she could have been so wrong. Totally unrepentant, his blue eyes twinkled back at her, and she watched in amazement as he checked his watch before pushing his fingers through his longish blond hair.

Obviously he was on a tight schedule.

"I loved being with you," he finally said. *"You're a very exciting woman, Amanda. The time we spent together was much more enjoyable than I'd originally imagined."*

"You planned this all along?" she asked, her voice shaking as the enormity of what was happening began to sink in.

"I planned to take over Mandy's Candies. The reputation you've built was a cherry I couldn't resist. The rest . . ." He shrugged and took a swallow of champagne. *"The rest was merely a form of negotiation. If you hadn't wanted marriage, I would have had to find another way."*

"Why is it so important to get me away from Mandy's Candies?"

A hint of steel sharpened his gaze. *"Mandy's Candies is my company now, sugar. Mine. I intend to run it my way, not yours."*

"You thought I wouldn't agree with what you wanted to do?"

"I knew you wouldn't."

"Amanda?"

Blayne's voice reached her through the mists of self-recrimination, and she turned to him with a sigh of apology on her lips. "I'm sorry, Blayne," she said. Remembering the other man in the room, she wondered what he thought of her lapse. In Tahoe Biff had dismissed Anthony so easily. *"You're angry, not brokenhearted."*

He was right. But at the moment she figured Biff was adding *stupid* to the description. She certainly deserved it.

She dragged a smile to her lips and continued. "It's just that I'm not ready to give up. I gave eight years of my life to Mandy's Candies."

"That's a long time," Blayne agreed solemnly, "but it's not as if you can't start something new with the money you got from the merger. The financial settlement you negotiated with Classic Foods was top-rate. You can do almost anything you want to now, including taking a rest if you're so inclined." His gaze widened to include Biff, and it was plain what he was thinking.

Amanda walked to his desk and placed her palms on the cool mahogany, leaning toward Blayne. "I'm going to get it back, Blayne," she said firmly. "One way or the other I'm going to get my business back."

For the first time in the long month that she'd been saying those words, Blayne looked as though he halfway believed her.

"Of course you are, darling," Biff said from over her shoulder. "Or should I say, *we* are."

Her head whipped around in surprise, and as she looked into Biff's eyes, she realized that he was totally convinced of what he'd just said. For the first time in a month she dared to believe. So she let that last "darling" slip by unremarked.

"For sure?" she asked.

"No guarantees, Amanda." His level gaze didn't flinch from hers. "No guarantees, but I can safely say we've got a good shot at it."

"How?" The word was a whisper that barely escaped her lips.

He grinned. "Now, that, Amanda, is what we're going to discuss over lunch." Standing, he tucked his arm around her waist as though he'd done it a thousand times, and said to Blayne, "Join us, counselor?"

THREE

Blayne made excuses not to join them for lunch on the grounds that he had another appointment.

On their way out the door Biff said he'd call on him in the next day or two to let him know what they'd decided to do. Blayne didn't look as though he wanted to know, but his curiosity apparently got the better of him, because he gave Biff his home number and told him to use it anytime, night or day.

Amanda couldn't imagine why Biff would need to speak to Blayne—*her* attorney—during nonoffice hours, but she was too absorbed by the pressure of Biff's arm around her waist to do much more than be grateful they'd be alone for lunch.

In fact it suited her just fine. She had a couple of things she was dying to ask the man who was walking at her side.

She waited until they were on the sidewalk and heading the direction of the parking lot before she slipped out of the circle of his arm. Blocking his path on the sidewalk, she stared up at him and wondered where to start.

"What's up, darling?" He cocked his head and smiled down at her.

"Darling?"

"I already told you how it makes me feel when you say that," he said smoothly.

She growled. "How dare you do this to me! Do you realize that Blayne is probably on the phone to Nancy this very second, telling her that a man—a man I've never even mentioned to her, or anyone else for that matter—just waltzed into a private business meeting and called me darling?" Her voice ended on a higher note than it had begun, and it didn't calm her down at all to notice that Biff's smile had widened.

"Nancy is his wife?"

Amanda nodded, thrown off balance by what she considered a mere detail in the larger picture she'd just described.

"Good." Biff edged closer. "Blayne didn't have a wedding ring on, and I wondered if I might have some competition there."

"Competition?" She shook her head sharply and re-applied herself to her attack. "Get back to the subject, Barley," she snapped. "What gives you the right—"

He reached out to touch his fingers to her lips. "Tell me you weren't glad to see me."

She couldn't. The anger she'd felt just moments ago evaporated into nothing at his touch, and all she could remember was the kiss he'd planted on her nose. Her mind swirled back to that electrifying moment a month ago when they'd been sitting so intimately, flirting with excitement . . . enjoying the danger.

"I was very glad to see you," she finally said. "Surprised, but glad."

A smile that looked suspiciously like relief curled his lips, and he nodded his satisfaction. He moved closer still and rested his forearms on her shoulders as he gazed into her upturned face. "I've spent four long weeks thinking about how exciting it was to be near you. I guess I've called you 'darling' in my mind so often, it became a habit. Sorry if I embarrassed you in front of your attorney, but I suppose I wanted him to know where I stood."

She laughed huskily, then her breath caught as his fingers began to stroke the nape of her neck. Lightly, slowly . . . The warmth of his touch sent shivers racing through her.

"Blayne's a friend," she said when she could speak without the tremble in her voice.

"I know that now," Biff said, his fingers working into her hair and tugging at the pins that held her chignon in place. "I knew it the moment you said 'darling.'"

"*You* said 'darling,'" she protested. "I merely repeated it."

"Whatever you say, darling."

Her sigh was only partly one of exasperation. "How long can you stay?"

"As long as you need me."

Her brows arched in surprise. "Don't you have to get back to Tahoe?"

"Not really." He chuckled at the bemused expression on her face.

"But I thought you lived there."

"I did."

"Did?" She was totally confused. Where did he live now if he'd left Tahoe? What kind of a job did he have that forced such changes?

"Did. I'll tell you about it later." He pocketed the

hairpins just as Amanda realized he'd pulled them all out. "In the meantime you're going to get a reputation for playing it fast and loose if we don't get off this sidewalk. If one more person walks by and pretends not to look, your reputation will be in shreds."

She didn't so much as budge. She couldn't, not with him standing so close, his body just inches from hers, his hands buried in her hair and working some sort of magic that left her paralyzed.

He laughed, a low, indulgent chuckle that curled around her soul and made her realize just how much she'd wanted to see him again. She'd tried so hard to forget, to get on with her life and the mess she'd made out of it.

But he'd come to her.

His eyes clouded with something mysterious and intense, and she knew he was going to kiss her. She wanted him to, needed him to . . . even went so far as to raise up on her toes to make it easy for him.

His mouth, firm and warm and tender, rested briefly atop hers, not so much a kiss as a concession to the need to touch each other there. For a mere touch it was dynamite. Amanda knew that he could hear the pounding of her heart because her ears were filled with its drumming to the exclusion of all else.

Then it was over. When he raised his head, she thought that maybe his ears were full of drums and whistles, too, because he looked as stunned as she felt.

"Lunch," he said shortly, clearing his throat and pulling her to his side once again. "And we'll use my truck, if you don't mind. I have a feeling that car of yours isn't going to be as easy to start as it was this morning."

She didn't even question how he knew what he knew.

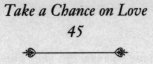
He let her choose the restaurant, claiming lack of familiarity with the network of small towns just north of Sausalito. Amanda didn't believe him because he seemed to know everything about everything, but kept her counsel and directed him to a popular restaurant in the town of Mill Valley. The Mill Grill was one of her favorite hangouts, the owner a friend of long standing. Jake had recently bought the restaurant, she told Biff, and had even more recently married. One of the by-products of his courtship of Mallory was an interesting collage that hung in the foyer. It had earned the distinction of becoming a local curiosity.

When she pointed it out to him, Biff grimaced and asked why someone didn't burn it. Pleased that they shared a distaste for that particular art form, Amanda hugged her friend Vincent—the restaurant manager and chef, who was gruffly acting the part of maître d'—and asked for a window table.

"Tell me more about Mandy's Candies." Biff leaned his forearms on the white linen tablecloth and gave Amanda his very best "I want to know every single detail" stare.

He might as well ask her to open her soul for his inspection, she thought. He couldn't possibly know how much of herself had gone into Mandy's Candies, nor how little she had outside of the gourmet-candy and petit-four shop.

She watched as he lifted a finger to stroke the scar on his face and wondered if he realized what he was doing. She wanted to know more about Biff, the man who made everything sound so easy, the man who *knew* so much about things she wouldn't have thought he'd know.

He knew how to touch her without touching. Every "darling" that he voiced was an electrifying stroke on her senses.

She took a sip of the mineral water she'd ordered, then set the glass down with a solid thunk. It was nonsense, the way she was reacting. He was just a man she'd met . . . a man she'd been so attracted to that she hadn't forgotten a single detail of the short time they'd been together. Nothing had changed since that hour they'd spent together in Tahoe. Nothing, including her attraction to him.

"I still don't know how you found me," she said instead of responding to his request. The solution to Mandy's Candies' problems could wait a while longer.

"That was the easy part," he said without any hint of a boast in his voice. "I had your name. I know people who know people . . ." His words trailed off, and she understood that the mechanics weren't important.

"But Mandy's Candies? How did you figure out what was going on? As far as I know, my severance from the company hasn't been announced."

"The *IJ* ran a small story on the merger," he said, referring to the local paper. "I also called Mandy's Candies this morning and found out you were no longer employed there. I pressed hard enough to discover you'd been fired."

It irked her that they were giving out that bit of information to whoever asked. "But how did you know to show up at Blayne's office?"

"I followed you," he said, and hid a laugh at her outraged expression. "After I called Mandy's Candies, I pulled up outside of your condo just in time to see you drive away."

"And you crashed my appointment." She shook her head in disbelief. "How did you know what I was doing there?"

He shrugged. "Guesswork, mainly. It was an attorney's office, and I figured it had something to do with Mandy's Candies."

"As easy as that?"

He grinned.

"Why?" she finally asked. "Why didn't you just wait until I came out?"

He looked genuinely surprised that she didn't understand. "I wouldn't have learned a damned thing standing out in the hall. How can I help you if I don't have all the facts?"

She snorted her disbelief. "For some reason I can't imagine a handful of details would get in your way."

He smiled serenely and picked up his menu as the waiter headed in their direction. "Would you rather believe that I couldn't wait another minute to see you?"

She blushed and wondered how much of what he'd just said was blarney.

None of it, she hoped.

She liked the feeling it gave her.

He grilled her about Mandy's Candies throughout lunch. She started with the year they'd turned a profit, and he made her go back to day one and describe how she'd begun it all. He was unrelenting with his thirst for details, absorbed by everything she told him. When they finished with the business aspects, he drilled her on the step-by-step processes for making candy. And petits fours. And everything else they did in the shop.

He wanted to know why she assumed Parks wouldn't maintain the quality standards for which Mandy's Candies was famous.

Amanda pushed aside her empty plate and folded her arms on the table. "When Anthony first approached me, I made it clear that expansion would only be successful if the same methods were maintained for production. He threw in some advice about reorganizing and using machines where practical, and I was vehement about not taking his suggestions."

She shrugged and took a sip of water. "To me hand-made chocolates and petits fours are exactly that—handmade. Introducing machines not only lowers the quality, but it makes a lie of the very thing for which Mandy's Candies is known."

"So he dropped the subject?" Biff guessed.

She nodded. "I thought he'd become convinced after seeing my operation." Her mouth twisted into a wry grin. "I imagine that's when he decided to dump me."

Biff agreed. "So you think he's going to install machines now?"

"Of course. It will take a few months, considering none of my employees are trained and such machines are probably custom-ordered, but I'm sure he's already got things in progress. Another month, maybe two, and he'll have exactly what he wants. A year from now, maybe less, when the customers begin to complain, he won't pay any attention because he'll have expanded the operation to cover up any losses."

Biff considered the point for a few moments before

asking, "Just what kind of expansion had you been considering?"

"More shops. More people. Mail order." She sighed and pushed her fingers through her hair in frustration. "The more famous Mandy's Candies becomes, the more business we generate. While finding skilled labor isn't any snap of the fingers, there is certainly enough out there to support the five or six shops I'd planned to open over the next few years."

"Parks's method will make Mandy's Candies famous," Biff pointed out.

She nodded sadly. "But it won't be *unique*, not anymore. It'll be no different from any other candy shop you see in malls from coast to coast."

He nodded his understanding. "Kind of hard to see something you worked so hard to build take a wrong turn."

"It's more than that." She leaned an elbow on the table and propped her chin on her fist. "Mandy's Candies has been my security for eight years. I guess I'm afraid that if I let it go, I'll lose everything else along with it."

"But I thought Blayne said you made out better than okay in the financial settlement," Biff said. "You've proven you can build a business out of nothing. What makes you think you can't do it again?"

She met his gaze with a determined one of her own. "It's not that I'm afraid to start over. It's just that I never thought I'd have to. I don't *want* to."

"People change jobs or careers all the time. In fact staying with the same company or career field is more the exception than the rule these days."

"Tell me about it!" she said with a harsh laugh. "My father probably holds the world record for the number of times he changed jobs. Why, I don't think he ever stayed anywhere long enough to earn insurance benefits or vacation time."

His brow creased into a frown. "You mean he got fired that often?"

"Not fired. He quit." She shook her head and sighed. "He was always looking for something better, something more interesting. It was like living with someone who believed in the pot of gold at the end of the rainbow."

"You don't believe there is one?"

She hesitated before answering. "I don't think it's something you find. I think it's something you make."

He smiled, and she felt the pleasure of his approval all the way to her toes.

"Still, darling, I don't think making a career change at this point in your life is going to put you in the same class as your father."

"You don't understand." She nibbled on her lower lip, trying to put together the words that would make it more clear. "It wasn't only that he changed jobs. We changed houses, towns, states. Nothing was the same from one year to the next. Mom and I followed him all over the place, and she was always promising me that next time we'd stay, make friends that I could keep . . . get through at least one year of school without the upheaval of moving."

"Did you?"

"Stay, you mean?"

He nodded.

"Not even once." She grimaced. "I think the record was the year I turned sixteen. Three jobs, two states, three schools."

Biff leaned back in his chair and waited for her to continue.

"I've built something for myself here with Mandy's Candies. I have a home and friends and know where to buy crab when it's out of season." A strand of hair fell into her eyes, and she blew it away. "The thought of having to begin all over again somewhere else takes away from that security."

"Security is a place?" he asked, surprise coloring his words.

She nodded, pleased that he understood. "Security is a home. Roots. A place to come back to."

A place to come back to. It was curious, Biff thought, the things people considered important. He didn't have to wonder what she'd think about his own lifestyle, where living out of a suitcase was at times a step up from what had come before. That was what he liked about his work—the freedom to go and live wherever he pleased and for as long as he pleased. Before Lake Tahoe it had been a sleepy town deep in the Maine woods. Before that a fishing village on the coast of Ireland.

He had no home base, unless he counted his parents' home in South Carolina, where he stored those things he didn't need with him at the moment. Not that there was much that needed storing. He'd never wanted to be weighed down by things.

He looked aside, studying the dock outside with its confusion of pelicans, gulls, and bay-side joggers. He'd promised to help her get Mandy's Candies back, and he would—even if it meant that by doing so, he'd be encouraging her to retreat once again to the controlled, insulated, *secure* world that she deemed so important.

For a moment he caught himself wondering what the

possibilities would be if she weren't so hung up on a home and hearth. They could travel together, he mused, to wherever the urge took them. They could hold hands beneath golden cupolas, discover foods that couldn't be found in posh ethnic restaurants . . . make love beneath the stars of a hemisphere she'd never seen.

He swallowed back the surprisingly vivid images of a future shared with a woman who so obviously had her own path to follow.

A path that led away from him.

The Amanda who sat across the table and talked about the security of home wasn't a woman who would be interested in climbing mountains or sailing seas, except for the odd vacation perhaps. Biff sighed and pushed away the disappointment he wasn't supposed to be feeling. This attraction between them wasn't going to be affected one way or the other by how they each viewed life and its rewards.

"My grandfather would have agreed with you," he said. "He was always so proud of the fact that four generations of our family had lived in the same house."

Amanda was just about to ask where that house was when he continued. "I suppose if he'd been around when I finished college, things might have turned out differently."

"How?"

Biff reached for the carafe of ice water and refilled their glasses. "He might have convinced me to go into the family business, for one thing."

She cocked her head and studied him. "Why doesn't that sound like something you wanted?"

He grinned. "Probably because it wasn't. I would

have done it, though, just to keep him from nagging me to death."

"He sounds like he was a big influence."

Biff stared at her for a moment, then said, "I loved him." He knew that she would understand.

"Tell me about him," she said, noting the faraway look in his eyes that was so obviously filled with fond memories. "What kind of business did he have?"

"Banking, mostly. A little real estate." He cleared his throat, remembering how easy it had been to walk away from it all once his grandfather had died. Easy, because he'd never really wanted to be part of it. It was his father he'd had to disappoint, his father who'd gone on to thrust the business into international prominence before finally selling out.

"My grandfather was always there for me when I needed him," he continued. "I wanted to do the same for him, but after he died, I just didn't see the point in doing something that really didn't interest me."

"I can't imagine you behind a desk," she said, resting her elbow on the padded arm of her chair. She cupped her chin on the heel of her hand and studied him. "What do you—"

He saw the question coming and headed it off with a shake of his head, not ready to give her an answer yet. What he did for a living could come later.

"We need to get back to Mandy's Candies," he reminded her.

"I suppose so." She smiled over the slow, weary sigh that flowed through her parted lips. It had been a long month, shadowed by worry and her anger over having been so foolish. Being here with Biff was a slice of heaven.

As she waited for him to speak, she wondered at the shrewd gleam in his eye.

"Have you ever considered going international with your unique little candy shop?" he asked.

"You're kidding, right?"

"Why?"

"You're looking at a woman who barely leaves her backyard for a vacation. Flitting around the world just isn't my style."

He studied her intently. "No vacations?"

"I can't. I won't. I don't." He looked so disappointed, she softened it. "Barley, I don't have an adventurous bone in my body."

Biff found himself wondering how she defined that night at Tahoe. As far as he was concerned, their encounter had been as exciting as any adventure he'd had, and he'd thought she felt the same way.

He forced a grin. "Of course I'm kidding about Mandy's Candies going international. But Parks won't know that."

"Parks?"

"You remember," he chided. "The man you were going to marry."

She shook her head in confusion. "I don't understand."

"That's the point, darling." He stood, then rested his palms on the table and leaned toward her. "Neither will Parks, and that's how it works."

"What works?"

"The con, Amanda darling."

"'Con.'" She thought about the word and the images it sparked in her. Chicanery, double cross, hustle. One of her favorite Paul Newman movies had involved an elaborate con. A frown creased her brow. "Are you suggesting we hoodwink Anthony into giving Mandy's Candies back to me?"

"Something like that," he said, then touched his lips to her cheek. "Let's go somewhere quiet so I can think about it."

Allowing herself to be led from the restaurant, Amanda wondered if Blayne had suspected something like this when he declined to join them for lunch. A con. It sounded vaguely illegal. Something akin to hope flared within her as she said a distracted good-bye to Victor.

"Give me a clue," she demanded as they crossed the foyer, impatient for whatever shred of hope he could give her.

Biff shook his head. "There are a couple of details I want to iron out before I tell you about it." Pulling her along behind him, he looked at her over his shoulder. "And then there's the matter of four and a half thousand dollars . . ."

FOUR

The money. She'd forgotten all about it. A queasy feeling overtook Amanda and nearly upset her balance as she followed Biff out the door. She should have known he wouldn't come all that way on an impulse to help a relative stranger. There was, after all, almost nothing between them—if one didn't count a bottle of champagne, a penchant for the word *darling*, a kiss in the sunshine.

Blinking rapidly against the glare of the early-afternoon sun, she slid a glance at the man walking beside her. "That's why you looked for me in the first place, isn't it?"

"Don't be silly, darling," he said, skirting a huddle of seagulls that were fighting noisily over a crust of bread. "I brought the money because I was coming to you. Not the other way around."

"Oh."

He grinned, and she felt his arm slipping around her waist in a gesture that was unsettling in its complete assumption of familiarity. It was as if she'd walked with him like this a dozen times . . . or a thousand. Amanda had heard it could be that way with some people—an instant connection that defied time or reason.

It was just that it had never happened to her. Not even once, and certainly not with Anthony. She stiffened, the fiasco of her recent engagement an open wound to her pride that had yet to completely heal. *She'd been such a fool!*

If Biff felt her resistance, he ignored it. His arm merely tightened ever so slightly when she tried to edge away from the too-familiar, too-disturbing embrace. She felt restrained, not captive . . . and she knew there was a big difference. Had she really wanted to, she could have simply walked out of the circle of his arm. She realized that, just as she knew Biff had merely checked her unthinking impulse to flee.

She was still trying to figure out how he knew what she was thinking when they arrived at his truck. His arm shifted, turning her to face him and gently urging her to lean back against the side of the truck. His lean body was just a heartbeat from hers, his arm hard and warm around her waist. It was so intimate, the feeling she got being this close—and so incredibly right.

"Why didn't you come back to me, Amanda? I waited."

She knew what he was talking about without asking. Tahoe, the night she'd left without saying good-bye. She gave a small cry of frustration that he insisted on knowing it all.

It was so soon. Too soon. "I was afraid . . ."

"There's no reason to be afraid, darling. Not of me. Not of us."

He moved a fraction closer, and she felt denim against

the silk of her stockings, the rasp of the stiff fabric as his legs firmly bracketed hers. Her breath caught in her throat as she held his gaze. Hot and wild, sensations poured through her body at his bold advance . . . yet they were nothing compared with the wildfire she felt when he leaned into her. His thighs were rock hard against her, his rigid arousal an unmistakable heat against her belly.

Her body responded without reservation, her nipples tightening beneath her silk teddy, arrows of heat striking repeatedly between her legs. She grasped his arms and found in the corded strength beneath her hands yet another source of the fire that was overtaking her.

He threaded his fingers into her hair. "How can it frighten you to know that I want to be with you so badly, I can hardly think of anything else?"

"It's not you," she whispered. "It's me. I shouldn't be feeling like this, not now."

"Because you're supposed to be licking your wounds from that bogus engagement?"

"Something like that."

"Tell you what, darling," he said. "I won't accuse you of wanting me because you're on the rebound, and you try to remember that you never loved Parks in the first place."

"How do you know I didn't?"

"I told you in Tahoe," he reminded her. "You were angry, not heartbroken."

She remembered.

His fingers were warm against her chin, their pressure a light insistence that she meet his gaze. "Did you miss me, Amanda?" he asked softly. "Did you lie awake at night wondering what it would have been like if you'd stayed?"

"Yes," she whispered, and said a silent prayer of thanks for the second chance. For four long weeks she'd known that in running away from Biff, she'd left something incredibly precious behind. It was just a feeling, nothing more, but one of such strength, she hadn't been able to shake it.

"So did I," he murmured, then his lips were on hers in a hard, demanding kiss that sent her senses reeling. It was over as quickly as it had begun, leaving in its wake unfulfilled needs and wishes. Dazed by the sheer power of the things he made her feel with just a kiss, a frustrated cry escaped her lips. She watched in confusion as his mouth curved at the edges, his totally masculine satisfaction blatant in the deep chuckle that rumbled in his chest.

"I liked it, too, darling," he said, his mouth hovering just a breath from her ear. "How much more do you need to know about me before we do it again?"

Her brow creased in puzzlement. "Do what again?"

"Kiss." Loosening his hold on her, he stepped back and folded his arms across his chest. "I don't want you half-naked beneath me when you suddenly remember that you don't know much more than my name and whatever my cousin told you."

The needs that had been left wanting by his kiss fed on the graphic image, suffusing her with heat and color and a yearning like none she'd ever known. In his arms she experienced a desire that was intoxicating in its intensity.

His confidence was yet another source of excitement.

"I'm not the woman you met in that casino," she said, suddenly worried that he might expect more from her than she was capable of being. "I'm not sophisticated or exciting or rash. I'm just plain Amanda Lawrence, who took a night off and played a role."

He shrugged. "Role-playing can be fun. I've done it myself on occasion."

"But I've only done it once," she said emphatically. "I'm peanut butter and bingo, Barley, not champagne and blackjack."

He shook his head, smiling. "Don't be any more of an ass than you can help, darling." His eyes were almost black with a sensuality she found impossible to look away from. "You're whatever you want to be. It's counterproductive to define yourself in terms of things."

"Then how should I define myself?"

"By your heart." He moved close again, shutting out the sun as he bent his head to within inches of hers. "Your heart and your soul."

It was a fantasy that intruded on her reality, the way he talked, the way he made her think. Listening to Biff, she felt brave and exciting and so very different from the woman she knew herself to be.

"What if my soul insists I'm peanut butter and bingo?" she asked, making one last attempt to set the record straight.

"I love peanut butter and bingo."

She wanted to believe him.

"Let's go home, darling."

Home. There is was again, the casual assumption that it was a place they shared . . . that he belonged there. It was extraordinary to realize how much she liked that idea.

"Home," she agreed. A moment later Amanda found herself seated next to a man who insisted he needed time to think.

He wasn't the only one.

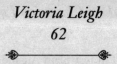

Biff leaned his forearms on the balcony's wood railing and enjoyed the view from Amanda's condo. Mount Tamalpais towered in the distance, its summit peaking above the low-hanging clouds that were a regular ingredient in the Bay Area scenery. Sunsets were magnificent, she'd said, given the clouds, pollution, and nearby ocean mists. He could believe it, and wondered what they'd be doing that evening when the sun went down.

His gaze dropped downward to where the tide was rushing into the lagoon below. Apparently it was the natural habitat of rays, seals, and all sorts of exotic-looking birds. She'd told him that if he was patient, he might spot a blue heron along the shore. Egrets were much more common, as were sandpipers and gulls.

With the exception of the Siamese cat he'd noticed prowling through the weeds, he hadn't spotted a thing.

They had taken the long way home, detouring through San Rafael to pick up her car. When the stubborn little Hillman had started with only a low growl of protest, Amanda had sighed her exasperation. They might as well drop it off at the mechanic's, she said, because something must be wrong with it if it started twice in a row without curses, multiple prayers, or any kind of fiddling under the hood. Biff didn't understand the logic, but when the mechanic appeared as concerned as Amanda, he decided this was some sort of prebreakdown ritual.

"There are soft drinks and seltzer in the fridge," she said from behind him.

"I'm okay, thanks." He looked aside and smiled as Amanda joined him at the railing. She had changed into a loosely flowing skirt and sleeveless T-shirt, both of them pale blue and soft-looking. Her feet were bare, and she'd pulled her hair back into a ponytail.

She looked about sixteen.

"How old are you, Amanda?"

"Thirty." She leaned her forearms on the rail and squinted into the sun. "Why?"

He shook his head and returned his gaze to the lagoon. "No reason. Just checking."

She sniffed her dissatisfaction.

"I'm thirty-four."

That earned him a look that was definitely amused. "Anything else you want to get off your chest?"

"Just filling in the blanks, Amanda."

"There are so many . . ."

He caught her gaze with his. "Ask me anything."

As if it could be that easy, she thought, and wondered how she could possibly make any sense of the questions that were swirling in her mind. She focused on the tie and sport coat he still wore. "Aren't you warm in that?"

"It's January." He grinned as his gaze narrowed on her own skimpy attire.

"It's also got to be sixty degrees out here," she returned. "We sometimes go entire summers without it getting much warmer than that."

"Is that so?"

She nodded. "Bay Area weather is notorious for being lopsided. July can be so foggy that you get lost crossing the street, while some of the most glorious days you'd ever imagine can pop up in October."

"Or even January."

His chuckle brought a blush to her cheeks as she realized they were discussing the weather. She sighed, shaking her head in self-reproach. So many questions, all of them important . . . or were they? Suddenly, without any sort of fanfare, the confusion in her mind settled into one tidy question.

"Why do I trust you?"

He looked at her curiously, not understanding. "I thought you and Blayne settled that?"

She shook her head. "I knew it before he made the calls."

Her simple words nearly brought Biff's heart to a standstill, pitching his emotions into a chaos that was dangerously enticing. It had been like that all month long, the anticipation of seeing her again a constant test of his control, his reason.

He'd never allowed a woman to affect him this way before. He wasn't sure he liked it. He sure as hell didn't understand it.

That night in the casino, he'd sensed something unusual in the way he reacted to her. The level of attraction between them went beyond anything he'd ever experienced before. The feelings she stirred within him were rendered almost unrecognizable by their intensity. He had followed her from Tahoe with a disturbing awareness that his life would never again be the same.

There hadn't seemed to be any choice.

"What's wrong?" she asked, her husky voice cutting across the thundering of his heart.

He shook his head. She trusted him without needing confirmation from anyone. That was enough for now . . . for both of them.

"Why *do* I trust you, Barley?" she asked again.

"That's something you're going to have to answer for yourself, darling," he said, flicking her ponytail back, his hand settling on her bare shoulder.

"It just doesn't make sense," she muttered. "I shouldn't, you know. Not after what Anthony did."

Listen to your soul, he silently urged her.

She worried her bottom lip with even, white teeth. "I learned absolutely nothing about you that night in the casino."

"Not my fault," he said, his fingers grazing the soft skin of her arm. "We'd hardly gotten acquainted when you left."

"You appear in Blayne's office out of thin air—"

"The secretary showed me in."

"You talk about tricking Anthony into giving back my company—"

"Blayne wouldn't have let me back into the office if he didn't think I could do something."

Her expression was suddenly grim and self-conscious. "I never thought of myself as vindictive."

He touched his thumb to her lips. "We're not going to do anything to Parks that he hasn't already done to you."

"I wish I'd met you before," she whispered. "It wouldn't have happened . . ."

Her lips were heating against the friction of his thumb, and Biff reluctantly moved his hand from her mouth. He found the ribbon that held her hair back and tugged it loose. "Look at it this way, Amanda. We might not have met at all were it not for Parks." Her hair fell around his hand in a heavy swirl, the sun-warmed waves an erotic stimulus to his imagination.

"I'd hate to think I owe Anthony anything."

"I don't want you to think of him at all."

"Why?"

Even as Amanda asked the question, she knew why.

Her heart stood still, then raced ahead as her desire for Biff swelled deep inside. She leaned against the hand that was buried in her hair and knew that everything of importance had been said.

She trusted him . . . and from that trust grew a sense of excitement that eclipsed any sensible questions.

"I want to make love with you, Amanda," he murmured, his eyes pools of black desire in which she saw reflected the startling intensity of her own needs.

"Okay," she said. And she smiled, a slow, sexy smile. "Come inside."

His voice was a low, husky invitation that tripled her awareness of the heady attraction between them. He held out his hand. She took it, and they left the mild afternoon breezes behind.

Her condominium was spacious and decorated in shades of white. The dining and living rooms were on the lagoon side of the building, with floor-to-ceiling windows straight across. A short, wide hallway led to the back of the apartment, where her bedroom and study were one long room with French doors between them. The kitchen was an airy sort of arrangement in the corner, brightened by a skylight and made extremely functional by a long bar with stools beneath it.

It was to those stools that Biff led her.

He put his hands at her waist, giving her the extra boost she needed to get seated. He waited until she relaxed against the cushioned back before moving away. She watched him, completely disoriented, as he tugged off his tie and threw it over the back of a nearby chair. His sport coat followed.

"What are we doing in the kitchen?" she asked as he turned back to her.

His lips curved into a sensual smile that took her breath away. "Use your imagination, darling," he said, then crossed to the china cabinet that was built into the wall. He opened the glass door and extracted two champagne flutes. Holding them in one hand, he went to the refrigerator, where he splashed a little seltzer into both.

"Even my imagination won't make champagne out of seltzer," she teased, but the humor left her abruptly when he pressed a glass into her hand and slid onto the stool beside her. The connection was made. . . .

Her hand was trembling as he gave her a glass, the white heat of awareness sparking between them as they touched . . . her fingers drifting across his, then sliding down to take the stemmed crystal from him.

"Remember the casino, when I tucked your legs between mine?" he asked, his voice a murmur that stroked her senses into a swirl of heat and wanting.

"I remember." Her fingers tightened around the fragile crystal as she found herself a prisoner of the excitement he created with only a suggestion. She watched, her heart pounding in her breast, as he set his own glass on the bar. His hands went to her legs. He pushed her knees together, bracketing her between his thighs, then slowly, carefully, pushed her skirt up her thighs. Her breath was coming less evenly now, the callused warmth of his hands a seductive pull she couldn't resist.

He stopped.

"It was about there," he said, looking down to check before returning his gaze to hers. "The dress you had on that night came up about that far when you sat down. I remember being half afraid that it would hitch up another inch and I'd see the tops of your stockings."

She gasped. "How did you know I wore stockings?"

Desire sizzled in his gaze, and he laughed softly. "I knew." He looked down again, and she watched mesmerized as he drew a long finger from her knee to the bunched skirt. "Did you have anything else on beneath that dress, Amanda?"

She only stared, her breathing coming more erratically now.

"Just panties, stockings, and garter belt? Nothing else?"

"No," she whispered, her voice thready with desire. "Nothing else."

He gave a low growl of approval but didn't look up. Both hands were on her thighs now, rimming the rumpled material with controlled, calculated strokes. "Do you know what I really wanted to do that night, Amanda?"

She could only imagine.

He didn't wait for her answer. His hands slipped between her thighs and pressed her legs open, holding them wide and inserting his own legs against her soft inner skin. He didn't think the denim of his jeans would bother her, but he was careful just the same.

He wanted to give her pleasure—as much as she could stand.

Biff looked up at her, his own excitement growing as he saw the total arousal in her eyes. He took the flute of seltzer from her fingers and set it aside. Leaning forward, he rested his hands on her thighs and brushed his cheek against hers.

"I wanted to touch you that night," he whispered. "There was such electricity between us, such excitement.

I couldn't help but imagine what it would be like to make love to you."

The fire nearly consumed Amanda, and they'd barely begun. What would it be like to have Barley for a lover? she wondered, not for the first time. It was time she found out.

Her hands were trembling, but she wrapped them around his neck anyway, not caring that he knew how deeply he affected her. She levered herself close to him, her breasts nuzzling his chest, their peaks hard, almost painful as they swelled against him. Her lips skated the bridge of his nose, his brow, his jaw . . . and finally his mouth.

She knew it was then that she lost control.

There was no tentative exploration, nothing polite about the kiss at all. He took her mouth and mated with it, his tongue stroking, caressing deep inside. His fingers threaded urgently into her hair, holding her head still for his mouth, then moving her a degree or so for better access. His lips were hard, demanding everything, teaching her erotic pleasures she'd never imagined existed.

Hungry and wild, it was like nothing she'd ever done before.

Amanda tasted like wildfire . . . and Biff was about ten seconds from taking her right there on the chair. It wasn't going to happen that way! Not the first time.

He wanted to take the time to show her how much he cared.

He stroked his tongue along hers, slower now, gentler, forcing the pace to lessen. It was painful, for her as well as for him if her frustrated cries were anything to go by. Soothing, meaningless words left his lips as he planted wet, tender kisses across her face. His fingers loosened in her hair, pushing carefully through the heavy waves until he could massage the tender skin at the nape of her neck.

"Amanda?" he said when he could breathe again.

"Hmm?"

"Any doubts?"

Amanda opened her eyes to find that his gaze reflected the heat she felt throughout her body. "Doubts?" she said quietly, then realized he wouldn't go on without an answer because he was that full of caring.

That full of honor.

She smiled. "No doubts, Barley."

"Why do you sometimes call me Barley and other times call me Biff?" he asked, touching his lips to her brow.

"For the same reason that you either call me Amanda or darling," she said simply.

"You could call me darling."

"And you could kiss me again." Her hands fluttered across his back, and she knew impatience as she'd never known it before.

He did as she asked, waiting only until they were both breathing somewhat evenly before he began it again. Differently from before.

More slowly.

Taking his time . . . taking his pleasure.

His hands left her hair, finding her thighs again, stroking them to the point where her skirt stood sentry. Then he pushed her skirt up and away, finding the soft skin of her thighs an irresistible attraction, the wet heat between them an appalling test of his patience.

He touched her there, holding her mouth with his kiss as he discovered how much she wanted to be with him.

And he knew that the fantasy he'd suffered that first

night had nothing on the reality of being with Amanda. She was responsive and hot and so totally desirable, he could hardly remember where they were.

His fingers slipped past the silk panties that were wet with her desire. Swallowing her moans of pleasure, he tested her silken sheath with a single finger. It was so hot and tight, he moaned aloud with anticipation. When he added another finger to his exploration, she fell back against the cushioned chair with a cry.

She moved against the rhythm he set, her hands buried in his hair, her calves lifting to wrap around him.

It was time.

Sweeping her into his arms, he soothed and comforted her as he carried her into the bedroom. It was even cooler back there, the afternoon sun a stranger to the shadows within. Biff carefully set her on the bed, tugging away her clothes and the bed's comforter before urging her to lie back on the pillows.

He felt her watching him as he stripped off his own clothes and knew that his urgency was matched. He came down beside her, glorying in the sensual texture of her warm, soft skin against his own as she arched into his body. He knew that he'd never before felt such pleasure.

He suspected that without Amanda he never would again.

FIVE

She'd never before felt such pleasure.

Amanda wound her arms around Barley's neck and searched out his mouth with her own. She felt his impatience in the way his tongue stabbed and thrust its way into her mouth. His hands were between her legs, stroking, spreading her thighs even wider . . . posing her for the final intimacy.

There was a moment's pause as he leaned over the edge of the bed. He snagged his jeans up from the floor and delved into a pocket for the foil-wrapped package he'd brought. She watched bemused as he slipped on the protection she'd failed to consider.

"Good catch," she said, the words riding unevenly on a gasp of pleasure as he leaned down to catch a nipple between his teeth.

He grinned. "I figured you didn't need anything else to worry about right now." He knelt between her thighs, his hands smoothing across her flat belly to rest lightly on her hips.

Amanda found her gaze caught and held by his. The amusement had gone as abruptly as it had surfaced. In its place was an almost desperate passion that she was quick to recognize as being the same yearning she felt to her very core. For a moment they both hesitated, as if it could be better with even the tiniest of delays.

A moment, no more. Murmuring arousing words of encouragement and praise, he tightened his hands around her hips and tilted her to meet him.

The love that they made together was unlike anything either had ever experienced before. More than sensation and pleasure was involved, although neither could identify that extra dimension that danced in their blood and made them burn. With the skill of lovers who'd met like this a hundred times or more, they kissed and caressed and stroked skin that was moist with the sweat of their passion. They laughed at odd moments because it felt so good, their joy was impossible to contain.

They moved together in a slow rhythm that defied the urgency of their need, since rushing was suddenly out of the question. Speaking in whispers, they vowed to make it last forever . . . or longer, if it were possible.

Forever, of course, was an exaggeration of intent that neither could be blamed for wanting. It was that good between them, an extraordinary joining of mind and body . . . a man and a woman celebrating life's most basic gift.

Later, after the fireworks and shooting stars had receded to occasional spurts of light, she asked him how long before they could do it again.

"Days," he said, panting hard as he licked a salty drop of sweat from beneath the curve of her breast. "Maybe weeks. My heart isn't strong enough to keep up the pace you set."

She giggled, her hand stroking the long line of his hip and beyond. "It's not your heart I'm asking about."

The part of him that wasn't his heart surprised them both and responded to her touch.

Amanda put her ear to his chest where she heard the distant thudding of a heart that was strong and willing. She smiled and opened her mouth on that exact spot.

The rhythm faltered, then she knew no more as Barley rolled her beneath him and proceeded to torture her for daring so much so soon.

Making love was every bit as delicious the second time as it had been the first.

He took her out to dinner that night because he wanted fresh crab and she didn't happen to have any in the refrigerator.

"I still don't see why you turned your nose up at meat-loaf sandwiches," she said after taking a sip of the dry white wine he'd ordered. "I happen to make a terrific meat loaf."

Biff folded his arms on the table and leaned forward, his eyes glittering with a wicked expression. "If we ate the meat loaf for dinner, than what would we have for a midnight snack?"

"I'm never awake at midnight," she returned, a blush rising in her cheeks as she realized he'd answered the question of where he was spending the night.

He chuckled, a low rumble that sent a shiver of antic-ipation down her back. "Want to make a bet?"

She was saved from answering by the arrival of the

waiter with their appetizers. The strong, heady aroma of garlic from the grilled shrimp she'd ordered made her taste buds water. Amanda quickly peeled one and popped it into her mouth. She was peeling a second before she looked up to see if Biff was keeping up.

He was. "Nothing like fresh seafood," he said, tucking a sliver of cold lobster into his mouth.

"Where do you live that you don't get any?" It should have unsettled her to realize that she was still unaware what he did for a living or where he lived. It should have, but it didn't.

She'd known quite a lot about Anthony, and look where that had gotten her.

"I've been living in Tahoe for the last year and a bit," he said, pushing his empty plate aside. "We do get seafood there, but it never tastes as fresh as when it comes straight from the ocean."

"But you mentioned earlier that you didn't live there anymore." She polished off the last shrimp and touched the stiff, white napkin to her lips. "Are you going to tell me where you've moved to, or is it going to be another mystery?"

"Mystery?"

"Everything about you is mysterious. Besides not knowing where your home is, I haven't a clue what you do for a living." She sipped her wine and frowned. "Then there are the more complicated questions."

"Such as?"

"Why do I have total faith that you will somehow find a way to trick Anthony into giving my company back to me, yet I don't have a single fact to back up that faith?" She took a deep breath and lowered her voice so that there wasn't a chance she'd be overheard. "Why do I trust you enough to make love with you, but . . ."

"But what, darling?"

But I don't have the slightest confidence you won't break my heart. She blinked against the sudden wash of tears that came out of nowhere.

Amanda shook her head against the question in his eyes and made up a new ending. "I trust you enough to make love with you, but can't for the life of me figure out why." Shutting her gaze to his, she focused on the glass of wine that she held and hoped he would let it go. She couldn't tell him what she didn't understand herself.

When he didn't respond, a part of her breathed a little easier. It was better this way, less complicated. Keeping her questions to herself would make his leaving easier on both of them.

She wondered when that would be. Soon enough, she figured. In the meantime, she was going to take advantage of the time she had.

A strength of purpose filled her with a warmth she knew was as much from the heart as from the soul.

I trust you enough to make love with you, but . . . Biff was curious to know what she'd really been about to say when her better judgment cut her off. More than curious. He hated not knowing what was going on in her head, the things that she didn't trust him enough to share.

He wanted her to know there was nothing she couldn't tell him, nothing she needed to hold back out of shyness . . . or pride.

Clenching his teeth against his disappointment, he tried to tell himself that it was early yet. Maybe in a few days she'd understand that there were no secrets between them. No lies.

"You're looking like the lobster bit back."

He looked up to find her watching him with an openly amused expression on her face. As he gazed at her, her eyes clouded in much the same way they'd done earlier . . . when he'd pushed up her skirt to discover the soft, wet curls between her legs.

"What's wrong, Barley?" she whispered. "Thinking we might have been better off with meat loaf after all?"

His stomach lurched at her teasing words. *Control*, he told himself as he took deep, calming breaths. It was incredible how easily she affected him with that sweet voice of hers . . . and how her smooth, strong hands had brought him to a level of ecstasy he'd never before imagined.

His body hardened in a totally erotic response, and he wondered if he'd always react to her like this, coming alive at the smallest provocation. If so, being with Amanda was going to take some getting used to.

He thought he could handle it.

"Barley?"

"Hmm?"

"What on earth is going through your mind?" She leaned back as the waiter whisked away the empty plates and refilled their glasses.

He cleared his throat, thinking that perhaps now was the time to tell her about his plan for Mandy's Candies. It certainly wouldn't do either of them any good if he were to put words to his actual thoughts. She'd get that look in her eyes that he couldn't resist, the look that told him her body was quickening . . . the look that begged him to touch her in those soft, silky places, so that she could show him how hotly she burned for him.

Amanda sprawled beneath him in all her sensual splendor,

*her hair fanned out on the pillow, his mouth following the path
of his hands as he—*

"Barley!"

He cleared his throat again and had to laugh at the
look of total bewilderment on her face.

"Sorry, darling," he said, and took a healthy swallow
of the wine. "I was trying to decide which question to
answer first." He let his gaze drift over her, taking time to
gather his thoughts as he appreciated her almost effortless
beauty. She had dressed for their evening out more
quickly than he. By the time he'd found the clothes he'd
worn that afternoon, Amanda had already pulled on a
wine-colored cashmere sweater and skirt, brushed her
hair to lie loose on her shoulders, and touched her cheeks
with a hint of color. She'd had to wait as he grabbed his
overnight kit from the car, watching with interest as he
shaved for the second time that day.

He'd never had a woman wait for him before.

"Why don't you start from Tahoe and work from
there?" she suggested.

"Actually I was thinking we'd talk about Mandy's
Candies."

She shook her head in exasperation. "Did you ever
notice how hard it is for you to talk about yourself?"

"Yeah." He grinned and changed the subject. "Now,
about your business, darling. It seems to me that we have
to make Parks decide that he wants nothing to do with
Mandy's Candies. If we can convince him of that, then
he'll exercise his option not to complete the terms of the
merger."

"I think I'm with you so far," she said dryly. "It may
not have occurred to you, Biff, but that exact thought has
crossed my mind once or twice over the last month."

He let that jab go by without comment. Leaning his arms on the table, he captured her gaze with his. "I know it's been a month filled with a lot of pain, darling. What have you been doing with yourself—besides worrying—since Parks took over?"

"What does that have to do with what we're going to do to get rid of Anthony?"

Biff shrugged. "Maybe nothing. Tell me anyway."

She was exasperated . . . yet flattered, because he was looking at her as though he was prepared to hang on to her every word.

It was immensely satisfying to capture the interest of a man as exciting as Barley, even if it was only for a short time. He would leave, she knew. Sooner than later, most likely. Not that she could give him any reason to stay that could compete with the adventures that beckoned to him. That he led an exciting life she didn't doubt, just as she knew he was accustomed to a world that was totally foreign to the small, safe niche she'd carved out for herself.

She knew him not at all . . . yet better than she'd ever known another man. It was a perplexing conundrum, which she blamed on her rioting emotions.

Amanda broke from his compelling gaze by lowering her lashes, then began to tell him what he wanted to know. The questions she'd asked him would just have to wait for later.

It wasn't as though he was giving her a choice in the matter.

"I've mostly just tried to stay busy," she said, thinking back to the beginning, that very first day when she'd awakened to face endless hours unchallenged by the demands of Mandy's Candies. "Since I was used to putting in twelve-hour days at the shop, sitting around the condo and watching soaps lost its appeal the first morning. Haunting Blayne's office wasn't an option either."

"He threw you out?"

She grimaced. "Something like that. Anyway I spent the rest of that first day in a café across the street from Mandy's Candies."

"Spying?" he asked.

"Sniveling." She colored at his quick laugh. "I was indulging in a massive dose of self-pity. It lasted all afternoon."

"Probably did you good to get it out of your system."

She shrugged. "Anyway that pretty much took care of Day One. The rest of the month was somewhat more productive. I repainted my condo, caught up on all the letters I hadn't had time to write before, took long walks, and read at least one book every day."

Biff gave her a quick grin of approval. "At least you weren't pining away for lack of anything to do." Then he asked her how to make petits fours.

Her eyes lit up with enthusiasm. She rested her forearms on the table and leaned forward. "With petits fours we start with my top-secret butter-cake recipe."

Biff listened carefully, not so much to the intricate description but to the tone of her voice. It confirmed what he already suspected. She loved what she did, actually relished the mechanics of concocting the sweets. It was extraordinary, because he knew that she loved the business end of Mandy's Candies as well. Most people enjoyed one end of a business and tolerated the other. Amanda loved both with equal enthusiasm.

"How did you get started?" he asked after she'd finished the petits fours and whisked him through truffles, tortes, and toffees. "Was your mother a dessert fiend?"

She rolled her eyes heavenward. "Mother couldn't cook her way out of a box. It was my grandfather who got me interested. He worked as a chef in New Orleans for most of his life, mostly doing pastries and candies. He would spend a month with us every summer—wherever we happened to be—and we'd experiment."

"Did he teach you everything he knew?"

"That, and he made sure I went to a good school where I could get a broader background." She fluttered her lashes in pretended exasperation. "He was afraid I wouldn't know anything more about food than the part that came after the entrée."

"Do you?"

She shook her head. "Cooking generally doesn't interest me if it doesn't have sugar in it."

"Then you weren't joking about the peanut butter, were you?"

"Or about the meat loaf either," she said. "While I might not go in for fancy sauces and complicated recipes, my meat loaf is world-class."

He smiled. "I'm looking forward to judging it for myself."

A midnight snack. Amanda found her gaze caught and captured by his, the sizzle of sex a luscious accent to something that was just beneath the surface of her consciousness, something she couldn't quite put her finger on. Her skin tingled all over, arrows of tension darting from her toes to the nape of her neck. Where just a moment before she'd been caught up in the excitement of sharing the joys of her work, she was now burning with a desire only Barley could satisfy.

He propelled her through the extremeties of emotion with no more than a look.

The waiter intruded then with two enormous plates of chilled cracked crab, and they were reluctantly distracted.

Amanda caught the look of annoyance that flashed across Barley's face and laughed. "We could always ask the waiter to put it into a bag."

"Or we could eat it now."

"If that's what you want," she said, giving in only because she was starved. Taking a crab claw in one hand and a tiny fork in the other, she dug out a succulent piece of pink meat and dipped it into the small tub of mayonnaise. She tucked the morsel between her lips and sighed.

It was as good as it had been the last time she'd had it—three nights earlier, to be precise. Fresh cracked crab, in season, was a delicacy she enjoyed at frequent intervals. The fact that there hadn't been any in her refrigerator had been a fluke.

They ate in companionable silence for several minutes, the only noises coming from an extremely happy Biff, who was taking great pleasure in dissecting the crab before him. He'd just finished the claws and was attacking the more difficult "heart" when a loud cheering erupted from the other end of the room. Like everyone else, Amanda and Biff found their attention diverted by what appeared to be a small gathering of Boy Scouts and adults. Two of the scouts were in the process of blowing out a number of candles atop an enormous cake.

"Wonder what they're celebrating?" she murmured, glancing at Biff in time to see a wide smile on his face.

"Looks like those two might have just received their Eagle Scout badges," he said. "Hard to tell from over here, but they're about the right age, and it's definitely an event worth celebrating."

"Somehow I knew you were a Boy Scout," she said with a smile.

"Still am." He grinned at her startled expression. "Well, kind of. I got involved with a troop in Tahoe last year. When I told them I was leaving, they couldn't decide whether they were saying good-bye to a scout or a troop leader."

"Which do you think it was?"

He shrugged and forked a small piece of the white, juicy meat into his mouth. "I figured they already had two leaders. What did they need with a third?"

"What indeed?" Putting down her own fork, she wiped her hands on her napkin and waited until he met her gaze. "So what were you doing in Tahoe, besides hanging out with Boy Scouts?"

Biff was so adept at not answering that question that the half-truth was out before he could stop it. "Working. My cousin has a hotel close to the casino where we met. I tended bar there for the last year."

"You're a bartender?"

"Disappointed?" he asked softly.

"Surprised. I wouldn't have thought that mixing drinks for a living would be enough for you."

"Bartending is a lot harder than it looks," he said, remembering the long hours of frantic activity that were matched by equally long hours of excruciating boredom. Bartending had been more of a challenge to his endurance than he'd originally counted on, and he'd had to push himself to the limit to keep up with his writing commitments when he wasn't on shift.

A flush of embarrassment colored her face. "Sorry

about that. I don't mean to sound like a snob. I spent enough nights during college waiting tables myself to know how hard that kind of work can be."

He smiled. "No offense taken."

A bartender. Amanda mulled it over as Biff resumed eating. It didn't fit, and she could point to a dozen reasons why not, beginning with the calm assurance in his manner when he'd pushed his way into her meeting with Blayne that morning. He hadn't been out of place in the attorney's office. On the contrary, he'd looked as if he'd been in similar places a hundred times.

There was more to this than he was telling her. There had to be.

"Would it make more sense if I told you I'm also a journalist?"

She looked up to find him watching her. "A journalist?"

He nodded.

"Why didn't you just say that in the first place?"

"It's not something I'm in the habit of telling people," he said, picking up his fork again.

"Why not?"

"Privacy and anonymity, for the most part." He poked at the delicate membranes behind which were hidden tiny morsels of crab. "I found out a long time ago that it's easier to do research if every Tom, Dick, and Harry isn't either trying to get his name into print or, worse yet, mucking with the facts."

"What kind of journalist?" This was more like it, she thought, her gaze thoughtful on his chiseled good looks. There was a wealth of experience in the lean contours of his face, much more than thirty-four years should have given him. As a journalist, she imagined, he lived harder than most, saw more than most. It made sense.

"Mostly I write long articles—thought pieces. Essays." Satisfied that he'd managed to ferret out the best of the crab, he dropped the empty cavity onto his plate and wiped his hands on his napkin.

"Where would I look to find something you've written?"

"I do free-lance work for several magazines." He named a few of them, including an esoteric travel magazine to which she'd been uncompromisingly addicted for the last ten years or so.

Her interest was definitely piqued, an understatement that brought a smile to her lips as she recalled the brilliant writing and gorgeous photos that filled the glossy magazine. Not that she actually went anywhere of course. Amanda didn't have the time or the inclination for anything more than the odd trip to the beach or the mountains. She wasn't the adventurous sort, she reminded herself. Curious about the world, but not driven to explore it. That was why she pored over the travel magazine when it arrived every month. Curiosity.

A thought flashed across her mind that Barley might be stretching the truth about writing articles, because she knew the bylines of all the regular contributors to the travel magazine, and Biff Fuller wasn't one of them. Neither was Barley Fuller. She shoved the thought aside with a distasteful grimace.

Barley wouldn't embellish the truth. He didn't need to.

"You don't write under Barley or Biff," she said matter-of-factly, dividing her attention between him and the crab on her plate. Setting aside the tiny fork, she used her fingers to expose the last bits of meat.

He raised a single eyebrow in surprise. "You're right. I use my given name—Bartholomew."

Bartholomew Fuller. Of course. The realization that the man she'd been fantasizing about for the last month was *the Bartholomew Fuller* was a shock to her system. Bartholomew/Barley/Biff was a world-class journalist whose travel articles gave her the sense of being across the world without leaving her living room.

Bartholomew/Barley/Biff was her lover. Somehow that little fact tempered the impulse to look at him any differently than she had before. The intimacy between them allowed her to see the man behind the legend and be comfortable with that image. All in all it took her exactly three seconds to get un–star struck.

Another two seconds passed, and she got just a little mad. How dare he keep this from her! Was he afraid she'd fall for the image instead of the man? Her anger percolated at the intimation that she might have already fallen for Barley. Or Bartholomew. Whatever. She fumed behind a shallow mask of imperturbable calm.

"Bartholomew Fuller. I should have realized . . ."

"You know my byline." Biff was surprised, because while many people recognized the articles, few took the trouble to discover who wrote them. He beamed.

She scowled. "Of course I know the byline Bartholomew Fuller. I've subscribed to that bloody travel magazine for over ten years."

I've subscribed to that bloody travel magazine for over ten years. He shielded his shock from her by looking down at his plate. It didn't make sense, not coming on top of her denial that she didn't, wouldn't, and couldn't take the time to see the world.

Food for thought, he mused. He looked up to discover her scowl had evolved into a glare.

"The same Bartholomew Fuller who wrote about the famine-relief effort in Ethiopia?" she asked.

He nodded. She was definitely aggravated. Aggravated and underwhelmed. He wondered if she was on the side of his critics.

"You wrote the essay on the disappearing bamboo forests in China."

"Yes." If looks were anything to go by, she hadn't liked that story any better. Biff was puzzled.

"The Bartholomew Fuller who put Pilau on the map?"

"It was already there," he said mildly, smiling because the tiny Pacific island held fond memories for him. "I just pointed it out."

She snorted. "Did you tell that octogenarian barnstormer who you were before or after you wrote the article about him?"

"Before," he said, then shot her a considering glance. "Would you please tell me if I'm supposed to apologize for who I am or for not telling you sooner?"

She ignored his question. "Which do you think I wanted, Biff? To get my name into print or muck with the facts?"

He winced. "Neither, darling. It's just such a habit . . ."

"You lied to me—"

"I never lied, Amanda," he said, wagging a finger at her. "Not technically. I really did tend bar."

Her raised brows told him what she thought of that excuse.

He rubbed his hand over the tense muscles at the back of his neck. "Any chance you're going to be reasonable about this?"

"I don't know," she said. "Maybe it depends on what kind of runaround you give me about the other easy question."

"What question?"

"Where is the great Bartholomew Fuller living these days?"

He grinned. "That's easy, darling. He's living with you." He stood up and turned over the check the waiter had left. From his pocket he pulled a number of bills, then held his hand out to Amanda. "What do you say to an Irish coffee before we go home, hmm?"

SIX

Shock was an effective antidote to anger.

Amanda stared at the glass mug in front of her and tried to pinpoint when it was that she'd lost her mind. Was it when she'd signed the contract with Anthony, or before? Had her thirtieth birthday signaled some sort of chemical change in her that screwed up any sense of what was real and what wasn't?

In the last month she'd lost her company, her job, and her fiancé. On the acquisition side she had Bartholomew Fuller for a roommate.

She was pretty sure things were getting just a wee bit out of her control.

"It's not like you don't have room, darling."

Barley's teasing words brought her head up with a jerk. "I think you're crazy."

"Does that mean yes or no?" He leaned back against the padded cushions of the booth and put an arm around her shoulders.

She turned sideways beneath his arm so that she could see his face. There was a mischievous glint in his eyes, discernible even in the dimly lit bar. She wondered if it meant that he was amused by her reaction to his announcement . . . or that he'd been teasing her all along.

Somehow, she knew he wasn't teasing, and her annoyance with him faded as quickly as it had arisen. "You really don't have a home, do you?"

"It's not a tragedy, darling," he said, a smile lighting up his eyes. "I just haven't decided where to go next." The arm that rested on her shoulders shifted, and he stroked her arm through her sweater. She settled back against him, wanting to comfort and be comforted.

"How can you be so blasé about it?" she asked. "I'd be in a state of panic."

"That's because you're comparing me to your father," he said roughly, cupping her chin in his fingers so that he could look into her eyes. "I'm not your father, Amanda."

"I know that—"

He cut her off. "I have a job that happens to tolerate a great deal of flexibility in my living arrangements. The more I travel, the more things I discover that I want to write about."

"Yes, but—"

"You told me your father was looking for the pot of gold, Amanda," he reminded her.

She nodded, well aware that she'd only get a word in edgewise when he was ready to let her.

"I'm not looking for gold," he said, his thumb rubbing across her chin. "I'm not looking for anything. I move around because I can. For now, with nothing to tie me down, moving is as easy as making up my mind and walking through the door."

Something that resembled envy rose up to startle her senses. Impatiently shaking her head, she batted it out of range. It was just that it sounded so carefree, the way he put it. Exciting even. Not at all like the uncertainty she'd grown up with.

"Did you come here because of a story?" she asked, her heart in her throat as she forced herself to meet his gaze.

He shook his head, then leaned toward her just enough to brush his lips across her forehead. "I came here because of you, darling. I thought you understood that."

The last vestige of anger disappeared under his gentle kiss. In its place was a curiosity she couldn't contain. "Where did you live before Tahoe?"

"Maine."

"And before that?"

"Ireland." His fingers gave her one last stroke, then dropped from her chin. He sipped the now lukewarm coffee and signaled the waiter. "In the six months that I was there, I occasionally helped out in the pub where the fishermen hung out. That's where I learned enough to convince my cousin I knew what I was doing behind a bar."

"Why do you take on other jobs if you're a journalist? It seems to me you'd have more than enough to keep you busy as it is."

"I like being around people," he said, then paused at the approach of the waiter. He asked for coffee without the Irish this time around, checking with Amanda before ordering the same for her. "It's also easier to get to know a place if you work in a visible job. People tend talk to you if you're a familiar face."

"Bartending is certainly ideal for that."

The waiter returned with the coffeepot, and Amanda waited until he was gone before saying, "Which of your jobs gives you the background for this thing we're going to pull on Anthony?"

He just grinned and shook his head. "Enough about me. Let me fill you in on the details of what we're going to do to that idiot Parks. Then maybe we can go home and not have to bring up his name again . . . at least not until morning."

"I hasten to remind you that I haven't agreed to let you stay with me." It was a deliberately provocative statement that dared him to say the things she wanted—*needed*—to hear.

He dared. "I don't want to sleep without you, Amanda," he said. "Give me tonight, give us tonight, and we'll talk about tomorrow when tomorrow comes. You need to know, though, that whatever you decide will make no difference to anything. I'll still help you." He took a deep breath and added, "I'll still want you."

Her gaze was drawn into the dark well of his own, and she found an honesty there that she couldn't resist. His softly spoken words aroused in her feelings of such incredible tenderness that she just stared at him, shivering beneath the arm that should have warmed her. The thought that he might actually stay away from her shook her badly.

"It's your decision, darling," he said.

"Please stay," she said quickly. "I need you." The admission wasn't something she'd planned on making, but it came out anyway, as if she had to match his honesty with her own.

He didn't say anything for a moment, but his arm tightened around her shoulders and his eyes darkened with warmth that she interpreted as approval. Then he smiled, a slow, satisfied smile that filled her with such pleasure, she could hardly contain it.

"Now, about Mandy's Candies—"

Her sigh was regretful, which was surprising because Mandy's Candies was supposed to be her focus, and she should have been eager to get started. She would have rather kept the conversation personal. Intimate.

She liked being intimate with Barley.

He ignored her sigh and began. "What if Parks was suddenly approached by an international hotel chain that wanted to put a Mandy's Candies shop into several of their locations? Don't you think that if they offered the proper incentives, it would be a cherry he couldn't resist?"

"I'm not sure anyone would be able to resist that," she said wistfully. "Assuming there was such an offer, though, wouldn't that make him even more determined to go through with the merger?"

"In the beginning that's exactly what we'll want him to think." Biff smiled, a feral grin that made Amanda glad he was on her side. "By the time we're finished with him, Parks will hand you Mandy's Candies and run like a rabbit to his hole."

Her pulse thrummed an excited response. "I think I'd like to have some details, Barley. Things like how many laws we're going to have to break while we're turning Anthony from an ass into a hare."

"Okay. First we have to convince Parks that someone on the international scale is indeed interested in Mandy's Candies. I know a guy who can get hold of some stationery from Paradise Hotels—they're based in Singapore. Anyway Wyatt Conner is an old friend who thinks he owes me a favor. He'll write the letter to Parks expressing an interest in putting Mandy's Candies in several of their hotels around the world."

"That's one," she said.

"One what?"

"Law we're going to break."

He shrugged. "As long as it can't be traced, it doesn't matter."

She wasn't sure she agreed with that, but decided to save judgment for later. Stealing stationery might be the least of her worries. "But what if Anthony decides to check back on the letter?"

"Parks won't do that, not at first." Biff took his arm from around her shoulders because it was so easy not to concentrate when he was touching her. Moving sideways in the booth, he satisfied himself with staring at the gorgeous picture she made in the dim light—her hair so soft and thick about her shoulders, her eyes sparkling with questions and interest.

Keeping his mind on the task at hand was a struggle, even at a distance. He continued. "Parks won't have enough information to worry about, not right away. The letter will be followed up by a call from Wyatt—"

"Where will he be calling from?"

"Singapore. That's where the headquarters is for Paradise Hotels."

"Wyatt is going to Singapore?"

Biff grinned. "That's the beauty of this. He's already there. I called him while you were in the shower."

Her brows lifted in surprise. "You talked this over with him before you told me?"

"No sense in getting you all excited before I had the details worked out."

"Thoughtful of you," she murmured, wishing he wasn't quite so distant. She missed the security of having his arm around her, the warmth that had nothing to do with hot or cold.

Later, she consoled herself.

"Anyway, Wyatt will get him excited about the deal. He'll throw out a few numbers, enough to make Parks agree to meet with him when he comes to San Francisco next week."

"Wyatt's coming to San Francisco?" she squeaked. "How am I going to afford that?"

His "I told you so" expression was unmistakable. "There's a check for four and a half thousand dollars sitting on your dresser doing nothing. I didn't think you'd mind spending it on a worthy cause."

Properly chagrined, she nodded and waited for him to go on.

"Wyatt will meet with Parks and hand him a detailed proposal that is so full of incentives, Parks won't be able to turn it down."

"Won't he be suspicious?"

"Parks knows that Mandy's Candies has a solid reputation in gourmet circles. That's why he wanted it in the first place. Wyatt will play on that, say something about Paradise Hotels only inviting top-of-the-line vendors. He'll tell Parks that the incentive package is designed to get things moving quickly. Paradise Hotels wants Mandy's Candies to open shop, and they want it now."

"What if Anthony decides to check up on Wyatt at this point?"

"No problem. He'll give Parks a business card with a phone number that goes somewhere besides the Paradise Hotel. The person on the other end will have all the right answers."

"And if he tries the number on the stationery?"

Biff paused for a split second before answering. "I'll remind Wyatt to mention that the number on the card is the real one while the one on the stationery is out-of-date. He'll tell Parks something about how they had to change the number because of new dialing codes or something."

"Pretty slick, Biff." She grinned. "We spend a couple thousand dollars convincing Anthony that Paradise Hotels will do for Mandy's Candies exactly what he promised me in the first place, except it's on an international scale. Anthony will like that."

"Wyatt will then give Parks a short turnaround on the proposal, say something about needing to fill the opening left by another vendor immediately. He'll demand a written commitment within a few days, setting the deadline for the day before you close escrow."

"But Anthony can't do that," she protested. "Legally Mandy's Candies won't be his yet. He can't sign stuff like that without my consent."

"True. But this will only be an agreement to do business once Mandy's Candies is legally his. Once Parks accepts, Wyatt will give him a token deposit—about ten thousand dollars should be enough."

"Isn't it normal for a prospective vendor to pay for the privilege and not the other way around?"

"Most of the time, but not all. In this case it will be part of the incentive package. Paradise Hotels will acknowledge that start-up costs, particularly overseas, might make Mandy's Candies less inclined to be enthusiastic. The money will be offered to help defray those costs and get things moving."

She nodded. So far so good. Except for one thing. "What happens to the ten thousand if I don't get Mandy's Candies back? The money will go into the business and never come out again."

"We'll make it a personal check drawn on Paradise

Hotels." He saw the objection in her eyes and held up his hand. "You can get checks made up with any name you want on them. I'll get some done here with the Paradise Hotels logo. Simple."

"Wouldn't Anthony ask for a certified one?"

"Not at this stage. It's not like they're going into escrow or anything."

She thought it sounded like he knew what he was talking about and wondered why that didn't bother her. "So Anthony gets a bum check drawn on a bum account. Won't he be just a little upset?"

"What do you care?"

She acknowledged his point with a quick grin, but persisted. Something—and she couldn't quite put her finger on it—didn't feel right. "Isn't there a chance that Wyatt could get into some trouble for forging checks or whatever?"

"If things go wrong and you actually lose Mandy's Candies for good, Parks will never be able to trace Wyatt." He sipped his coffee and smiled. "Trust me, Amanda. We need the routine with the money to clinch the deal. Without it Parks might feel he can tear up the agreement and walk away. But if he's taken their money, it will be impossible to back out and pretend it didn't happen. That's one of the things he's going to have to understand if this is going to work."

She had to admit that it made sense. "So tell me about this agreement."

"There won't be much to it. Just a few pages that look official and make him think he's legally committed to something."

"How do you know he'll sign?"

"I'm counting on his greed. Everything you've told me about Parks indicates he'll jump at this."

"You're right." Shaking her head in stunned admiration, she couldn't help but give praise where it was due. "I've got to admit it. As far as I can see, you've got all the bases covered."

"Glad you approve." Biff stretched out his legs beneath the table, found her ankles with his calf, and began to rub against her in pleasant rhythm.

"So what is going to make his little bubble burst?" The friction of his jeans against her stocking-covered legs was an erotic promise she found difficult to ignore. No, *ignore* wasn't quite the word. She could no more ignore the gentle abrasion than she could stop looking at him. He was looking back, his expression suffused with a kind of heat that made her want things she'd never wanted before.

Biff sighed regretfully and forced himself to continue. "This is where you get a chance to play a part. We arrange for you to run into Parks after his meeting with Wyatt—*after* he banks the check."

"What makes you think he'll race right out to the bank?"

"We're talking about a check drawn on an overseas bank by a man you've agreed to begin doing business with as early as next week. Wouldn't you want it to clear as fast as possible, just in case?" She was still hesitating, so he added, "Parks is a businessman. He won't spend a dime until that check has cleared and the money is in his bank."

He waited for her nod of agreement before continuing. "When Parks sees you, he won't be able to stop himself from bragging. That's when you go into your act. Remember what you told me about Tahoe, that you were playing a role?"

"I remember."

"This part is almost as good. Once Parks has accepted the hotel's proposition, you will confront him with the knowledge that he's getting involved—*is* involved—with people who shoot first and ask questions later. People with serious connections to drug trafficking."

"And he's supposed to believe me?" she asked, her half smile a perfect match to the incredulous expression in her eyes.

"He'll believe you," Biff said with complete confidence. "He'll be too scared not to."

Amanda took a deep breath and focused on the candle that burned between them, trying to regain a sense of perspective. It was hard, though, because she could almost taste the excitement. She felt herself being drawn inexorably into the spirit of what felt like the adventure of a lifetime. She'd never done anything remotely like this, nothing that ever felt so dangerous and so wonderfully thrilling at the same time.

"I think I had more faith that this was going to work before you told me what you had in mind," she said carefully. "How exactly am I supposed to pull this off?"

"We'll have to work on your approach, but basically the information that you have to get across is that Paradise Hotels approached you last year with the same offer . . . and you turned it down."

"Now, why would I do that?"

"Because, contrary to recent behavior, you actually consulted your attorney. He discovered that Paradise Hotels has very definite underworld connections—drug money, to be specific. Blayne advised you to stay away. He figured they want Mandy's Candies for some drug-related purpose, trafficking, money laundering, whatever. You don't have to be precise to get the point across."

"And Anthony panics, because he's just signed some sort of commitment to do business with drug lords." She grinned.

"He's also taken their money. You just need to let him know he's in big trouble." Biff straightened in his seat, fishing his wallet from his pocket to pay the tab. "If Parks has any brains at all, he'll realize that the only way out is to back out of buying Mandy's Candies. He'll figure that you'll be stuck with the agreement with Paradise and that they'll leave him alone."

"But what if he gets suspicious?"

Biff stood and pulled her up from the booth. "He won't have time. That's why you do your act the day before escrow closes. He won't have time to do anything but worry."

Standing, she tilted her head and smiled up at him. "You know something, Barley?"

"What?"

"This just might work."

"Of course it will." He kissed her, a brief, hard kiss that didn't begin to satisfy the growing need within him. "Trust me, darling. I won't let you down on this. Between you and me and Wyatt, we'll have Parks so tied up in knots, he'll never get himself untied."

"I've *always* trusted you, Barley." She smiled and raised up on her toes so that her mouth was a breath away from his. "I've just never known why."

Amanda was a restless sleeper, but that wasn't what was keeping him awake. She rolled away from him, taking most of the covers with her. Biff tugged on the quilted comforter until he had repossessed enough to keep himself warm, then reached over to pull it off her face and tuck the top edge under her chin. She made little noises in her sleep, nothing that he understood, but he listened carefully just the same.

Trust. She gave it without conditions, a gift of such precious value that it stole his breath. It wasn't just a word to her, a meaningless phrase that she'd heard somewhere and wanted to try out for effect.

She trusted him.

He loved her.

Amanda turned back toward him and inserted her knee between his thighs, murmuring incomprehensible sounds again as she snuggled her face into the curve of his shoulder. He groaned under her provocative assault, feeling his body harden even though he knew she was sound asleep and totally unaware of what she was doing. Still, his arms encircled her, drawing her closer so that he could feel the steady beat of her heart against his chest.

He loved her.

His ragged sigh was a surrender to a truth that settled on him with a comforting lightness, and he knew he must have suspected it all along. That first moment in the casino when she'd lifted her gaze to his, there had been a sense of bonding that neither had been able to explain.

"What were you looking for?" he asked.

"I don't know," she said, her voice a thready whisper. "It isn't something I can really explain. I just looked up because I knew you were there."

"You knew before you looked?"

She nodded. "And I felt . . ." Her words trailed off, her eyes clouding with confusion.

"You felt what? What did you feel?"

She stared at him in bewilderment. "I think . . . I felt the same thing you did."

Had it been love, even then, before they'd spoken a single word? Was such a thing possible?

Or was he going out of his mind, losing his sanity to some exotic disease that had lain cunningly dormant for just the right time, rising up and infecting him the exact moment he saw Amanda?

Sane or not, he wanted to be with her forever.

Love. He should have known. . . . Swearing under his breath, he stroked her hair and wondered if she had any idea how complicated things were about to get.

Closing his eyes, he held the woman he loved close to his heart and relegated the complications to hell.

SEVEN

He awakened Amanda with the rising sun.

She lay sprawled on her back, arms thrown above her head, her hair a tangle of curls across her face and pillow. He'd been awake for an hour, watching her as she shifted and mumbled in her sleep, forcing himself to wait because it hadn't been that many hours since they'd last made love.

His hands found her beneath the comforter, smoothing across the warm skin of her belly, gliding lower to discover her open thighs. His touch was light, a glancing caress across the springy curls that guarded her womanly secrets. He parted her with his fingers, stroking with gentle precision until he felt the slick welcome of her response. He was careful, not wanting her to awaken too soon, too suddenly.

She stretched, a catlike extension that trapped his hand between her legs and shifted the comforter to reveal her breasts. His breath came in harsh pants as he waited for her to open her eyes. Instead she murmured something and eased back against the pillows, her legs parting once again.

She was still asleep.

The nipples of her breasts were taut, whether from her unconscious arousal or the early-morning chill he wasn't sure. Either way they were too tempting to ignore. He opened his mouth over one, heating the hard nub with his breath before fastening his teeth around it.

Her breath hissed between her teeth, and he knew that she was with him. He growled a husky "Good morning" against her breast, and his fingers stroked with delicate persistence the part of her that was hot and moist with her arousal. Her hips rocked to meet him, and he sucked lightly on the distended nipple before leaving it. He found the other and began again—warming, biting, sucking.

She cried aloud and thrust her hands into his hair, telling him without words that she found pleasure in what he was doing. Her breast swelled beneath his mouth. He pushed two fingers deep inside her, stretching her, taunting her.

She was more than ready for him. Soft, incoherent words reached him as he eased his hand from between her legs. She writhed beneath the covers, her hands finding him, stroking the length of his desire until he could stand it no longer. Reaching across her, he found the foil packet that was on the bedside table. Her urgency made him clumsy, and in the end it took both of them to manage the job.

He rolled onto his back and took her with him, parting her legs over his thighs, lifting her by the hips so that only the very tip of his arousal touched her.

He held her there, ignoring her protests as he took his pleasure in the erotic picture she made—her hair falling in wild disarray about her shoulders, her breasts full and reddened from the rasp of his unshaven face, her eyes wide open, bright with the flames of her passion.

He held her poised above him until he could wait no longer. Slowly, steadily he entered the passage that led to her womb. He watched her face for any sign of discomfort—she was so tight, it was too soon after the last time. All he saw was an expression of such pleasure, his own was intensified almost beyond measure.

And that was only the beginning.

They spent the morning composing the letter. It was straightforward and to the point, giving Anthony an outline of Paradise Hotels' intentions regarding Mandy's Candies and little else except a request that Anthony meet with Wyatt the following week when he came to San Francisco on other business. Wearing only his jeans, Biff typed out the final draft on her personal computer, then sipped coffee as he waited for the hard copy to come off the printer.

Amanda grabbed it before he had a chance. Crossing to the window where the light was stronger, she skimmed through the text. The typed name at the bottom caught her attention. "Wyatt Conner, CEO?"

"Chief executive officer," Biff supplied, switching off the equipment and coming to stand behind her.

"I know what it means, Barley," she said, a note of exasperation in her voice. "What if Anthony knows the name of the real CEO of Paradise Hotels?"

Biff put his arms around her waist, his hands slipping inside the terry-cloth robe she wore to fondle her breasts. "Do *you* know the name of the CEO of Paradise Hotels?"

She shook her head, arching her neck as he nuzzled a spot below her ear. It was hard to think when he was doing that, but she persevered. "That still doesn't mean Anthony won't."

"Unlikely," he said, fastening his teeth around the lobe of her ear. "From what I understand, the guy is pretty low-profile. And since he doesn't own a single property in the United States, very little about the company is reported in the American press."

It made sense. She luxuriated in the sensations of erotic foreplay that Barley was so wonderfully skilled in, a gasp of pleasure parting her lips as his fingers danced provocatively across the tips of her breasts. Where he touched her, she burned. Her hands reached behind her to find him, wanting to know if he was as aroused as she.

He was. With a sigh of regret he backed off, pinching her nipples lightly before extricating himself from the folds of her robe.

"I've got to fax this to Wyatt," he said. "Why don't you get dressed and we'll go do something fun this afternoon."

She knew there was a certain wildness in her eyes as she spun to face him. "You're leaving? Now?" she asked incredulously. "How can you do that?"

"Not easily," he admitted, clearing his throat as he raked unsteady fingers through his hair. "There is a small matter, though, of needing to stop by the drugstore while I'm out."

It was then that she noticed the bulge in his jeans that betrayed his own discomfort. "Oh," she said, the hint of a smile curving her mouth.

"Yeah," he snorted, turning to walk through the French doors that led to her bedroom. "'Oh' is right."

She followed him, a giggle sneaking out before she could stop it. He shot her a dark look, which was sufficient to keep any further amusement muffled. Leaning against the dresser, she watched as he pulled a pink-and-beige-striped shirt out of the garment bag he'd brought in the night before and shoved his arms into it. Before buttoning the shirt, he rubbed a hand across his chin as if he couldn't remember whether he'd shaved that morning.

He had. She remembered because she'd stepped out of the shower to find him rubbing the mist from the mirror so that he could see to wield his razor. He'd kissed her then, shaving foam and all, a quick, hot kiss before turning back to the mirror.

She remembered.

"So what kind of fun am I supposed to get dressed for?" she asked as he stood in front of the mirror and dragged a comb through his hair. She hadn't meant to be so deliberately suggestive in her choice of words . . . or had she? Amanda watched as his shoulders tensed and knew she'd pushed a button that might have been better left untouched.

He put down the comb, his gaze finding her reflection as she stood behind him. She waited, her mouth dry from the unmistakable look of desire in his expression, her heart pounding so loudly that he couldn't help but hear it.

"Amanda?" he finally said, his voice a low growl that sent shivers up her spine.

"Yes?"

"You tempt me beyond anything that makes sense." His gaze traveled down her body before returning to her face. "I want to take you now, where you stand. The dresser isn't the most comfortable piece of furniture to make love on, but it will do. I want to feel your legs around me as I thrust into you. I want to hear those little cries you make when you're coming."

Biff took a deep breath, his hands clenching at his sides as he struggled against the desperate urge to go to her and follow through with the fantasy he was describing. "Did you know that when you tighten yourself around me, it drives me wild? It's like nothing I've ever felt before, the way you hold me so deep inside of you."

He watched her reactions and knew that she was as excited as he. Her fingers clutched the edge of the dresser. Her breathing was shallow and harsh, her eyes clouding with her desire as she returned his stare.

He tore his gaze from her reflection and picked up the comb. "Getting pregnant should be a choice, darling. Not a consequence." A shudder wracked his body as he fought to control himself. The image of Amanda pregnant almost tore through his resolve. Children with Amanda. A family.

There was so much more to loving than making love.

"Pregnant," she murmured. It was a whisper of a sound, no more, but it exploded into the room between them, fragments of emotion tearing at her in a way she couldn't even begin to understand. She saw the way he tensed, his hand pausing midair with the comb, and knew that she wasn't the only one affected.

"Is that what you want?" he asked softly. "A baby?" He set the comb down and turned to face her, crossing his arms on his chest.

Pregnant. A baby. Amanda shook her head until it rattled. She was confused, breathless . . . a lot like she'd felt that night at the casino in Tahoe. One moment they'd been talking about why she wanted to lose at blackjack, and the next she'd been sitting with her legs wedged between his as he introduced himself.

Barley moved with a speed that left her winded.

"Why is it that everything is so fast with you?" she asked. She smiled as she spoke, because, winded or not, it was so incredibly intoxicating just to be in the same room with him.

"You don't want children?" he asked, a hint of mischief lighting up his eyes.

She scowled, her fingers digging into the dresser at her back until she was sure she was making little dents in the wood. "I'm not going to stand here discussing children with a man who doesn't even have an address."

Biff blinked, surprised by her non sequitur. It wasn't so much that she'd connected children with having a home. What astonished him was the implication that it was only his homeless state that kept her from discussing the matter.

Interesting, he mused. "Are you saying I can't be a father because I'm temporarily between homes?"

The furrow between her brows deepened. "Don't put words into my mouth, Barley."

"But you said—"

"I said the first thing I could think of," she sputtered. "How can you bring up the subject of babies and expect me to think straight?"

"It was just a question, darling," he murmured, returning her smile with sigh. "The way you said the word *pregnant* made me think you might not be averse—"

She cut him off again. "Don't you have somewhere to go?"

He grinned, then bent down to feel under the bed for his shoes. He found them and whistled as he sat down and pulled them on. She was confused now, but he thought there might be an inkling of a feeling that was deeper than mere trust in the way she responded to him.

Standing up, he resisted glancing in her direction and walked into the adjoining room for the letter. He folded it and stuffed it into his pocket, then shrugged on the jacket he'd left draped over a chair. He'd be gone for an hour, maybe less. Walking back into the bedroom, he found Amanda where he'd left her, a scowl still on her face.

"Don't worry, darling," he said, coming to stand in front of her. "I'll be very careful not to get you pregnant."

She groaned, her head dropping to fall against his chest. "That's not what worries me, Barley."

"Then what is it?"

She lifted her head and met his concerned gaze. "I feel like I'm losing myself in you. You touch emotions in me that I didn't even know I had. I'm so afraid that when you leave, I won't feel these things ever again."

His heart thudded in his chest, and he wondered if she had any idea of the hope her simple words brought him. His hands framed her face, his fingers threading into her hair as he searched his heart for the words that would ease her fears.

"How can you be so sure I'll leave?" he asked.

For a moment there was a look of such joy on her face that he nearly told her he loved her. But it vanished as quickly as it had appeared, replaced by a self-deprecating smile. "Oh, you'll leave, Biff," she said. "It's not in your nature to stay anywhere, now, is it?"

He agreed, but couldn't help but think it was rather presumptuous of her to say as much. He'd never told her that he didn't want to settle down, just that he hadn't. But how could he tell her that he'd live anywhere as long as it was with her?

She wouldn't believe him.

"Does this mean you're not going to make me find another bed tonight, Amanda?" he asked, skirting the issue she'd raised with a finesse he hoped she wouldn't notice.

She looked at him long and hard before nodding. "You can stay. As long as you need to."

His relief manifested itself in a long, thankful sigh. He would stay, at least until they got Mandy's Candies sorted out. Anything after that would be up to Amanda.

"While you're out, would you swing by the store for oranges?" she asked. "As long as you're staying, I'll let you squeeze us some juice for breakfast."

"We already had breakfast, remember? You yelled at me for getting crumbs on the sheets."

"I'm talking about tomorrow," Amanda murmured, ducking her head to hide the rising heat in her cheeks. Oh, yes, she remembered breakfast. Biff had brought it to her in bed—if toast and coffee could really be called a proper breakfast. And then he'd proceeded to distract her with wicked suggestions of what they'd do if she ever finished eating. When she'd refused to be rushed—more out of obstinacy than anything else—he'd drawn the sheet from her body and proceeded to taunt her with lightning strokes of his hands and tongue that had made her forget about breakfast altogether.

She heard his laughter and knew he hadn't forgotten either.

"I won't be long, darling," he said, sliding an arm around her waist to bring her hard against his chest. He waited until she looked up at him, then kissed her gently.

"And don't bother to get dressed. We've got time to play out that fantasy I was telling you about before we leave."

She gasped, her face flooding with renewed color in that brief moment before he bent down to kiss her again. "I'll hurry," he said, and was gone before she could ask if he even knew where he was going.

Of course he did. A strange town wasn't a challenge to a man like Bartholomew Fuller. Not having a clue where he was going probably didn't even put him off his stride. Thinking that she had at least an hour before he found his way back, Amanda wandered into the kitchen and poured herself another cup of coffee. Taking it out onto the balcony, she made herself comfortable in a deck chair and stared determinedly at the lagoon.

Bird-watching was infinitely preferable to wondering why she couldn't let go of the feeling that Biff wanted more from her than she'd already given him. Much more.

A flash of white caught her attention, and she focused on her first sighting of the day. An egret, not uncommon at all but a beautiful sight that never failed to thrill her. Brilliant white feathers atop long, spindly legs, the egret was a relative of the equally graceful but rarer blue heron.

Pregnant. Babies. Children. Odd, really, the subjects that came up when she was around Barley. A sensation of restless longing surged through her, then was promptly subdued by the knowledge that he would never stay in one place long enough to create the family he made her want.

She couldn't help but wonder, though, what had prompted him to pursue such an intimate discussion. Most men would have shied away from the subject with a swiftness only matched by Olympic-class sprinters.

But, then, Barley wasn't like most men.

He was unlike any man she'd ever met.

Amanda sipped her coffee and stared without seeing at the heron that strutted along the opposite shore.

They lay together in the dim room, her breaths gradually becoming more even, his heart thudding erratically under her ear.

It got better every time they did it.

"Practice," he said.

"Expectations," she insisted. She expected their love-making to be wonderful, and he'd sworn never to let her down.

That wasn't what he'd been talking about.

Amanda pressed an open-mouthed kiss on his chest and slid off the bed, evading his last-minute grasping hands. "Rest," she told him, a deliberate teasing note in her voice. "Get your strength back."

He mumbled something about deserving the break, what with the extreme difference in their ages.

Four years. She grinned and wandered naked into the bathroom. After turning on the shower, she looked in the mirror for some sign of change. The same woman she'd come to recognize over the years stared back at her. Same eyes and nose. Same teeth. Same skin.

What did Barley see that made him want her with such passion? She shook her head and knew that she had to set him straight.

Bartholomew Fuller needed more out of life than peanut butter and bingo. He knew it. She knew it. It was time to remind him.

Before she fell in love with him. Before he walked out of her life for good.

Now . . . before it was too late.

She would show Barley who Amanda Lawrence really was. Not exciting, nor beautiful, nor even very interesting—at least not by Barley's standards. She showered, then nudged him out of bed so that she could have the privacy of her bedroom. While he was in the shower, she pulled on a pair of sweats that bore a strong resemblance to another half-dozen sets in her closet. The sweats were baggy, discolored, and decidedly nonflattering.

They were her wardrobe of choice when she was alone.

No makeup, no perfume. She did, though, brush her hair, three quick strokes followed by a rubber band to hold it out of her face.

Vintage Amanda. She avoided looking in the mirror on her way out of the room.

In the kitchen she made herself a peanut butter sandwich. At the front door, she slipped her feet into the sneakers that she'd dumped there a few days earlier and trotted down the stairs. Two minutes later she was sitting at the end of the public dock that edged out into the lagoon.

Biff padded across the thick carpet of the living room and peeked into the kitchen. She wasn't there either. He'd already looked in the study.

He wanted to tell her he loved her. First, though, he had to find her. He walked out onto the deck and spotted her down below. She was feeding the ducks. Half a dozen were swimming at her feet.

It looked like fun. He found his shoes, pulled on a knit shirt, and ducked back into the kitchen for the loaf of bread she'd left on the counter. He grinned when he saw the jar of peanut butter there, too, and wondered if she would be willing to change brands. He preferred another and wasn't about to change.

Then again, there wasn't any reason they couldn't buy both. He could afford it. So, for that matter, could she.

Whistling under his breath, he went out to join her. He immediately noticed she was eating more than she was giving away.

"I suppose peanut butter isn't on their diet," he said, easing down beside her to dangle his legs over the edge of the wooden dock.

"I was only giving them crusts."

He thought it was curious that she didn't look at him. "I brought more bread. From the deck it looked like you had more takers than supplies on hand."

"Thanks." She took a couple of slices from the bag and tore them into small pieces that she gathered in a fold of her baggy sweatshirt. Once she had a substantial pile, she tossed them in one throw onto the water. Biff watched as the ducks sparred for the treats, a few seconds of frantic activity before the surface of the water was empty save for the feathered diners.

She took two more slices and did it again, all without looking at him. Something was worrying her. He didn't have to see her expression to know that.

"Would you rather I went back inside?" he asked after the third throw.

That at least earned him a glance. He held out two more slices of bread and waited for her answer.

"You can stay if you like." She turned back to the water. "I won't be much longer. I need to get some things done around the house this afternoon."

"Anything I can help with?"

She shook her head. "Thanks, no. I just want to do the laundry, change the sheets. Housework."

"I do windows."

The look she gave him was disbelieving. "Somehow I can't imagine the great Bartholomew Fuller lowering himself to scrub floors."

So that was it, he thought. Amanda was back to blackjack versus bingo. He should have known the peanut butter was out for a reason.

"I said windows, not floors," he kidded, just in case there was the slightest chance he could tease her out of this bizarre mood. "And I don't mind dusting if you're not too picky about where knickknacks go when I'm done."

Silence.

"I like feeding ducks too."

She spoke without looking at him. "Biff, you need to get your facts straight. You lead a glamorous, exciting life. I don't. With the exception of Mandy's Candies, my life is dull by your standards. I stay at home a lot, wear comfortable clothes and no makeup. I do my own housework and use the good china on special occasions—about twice a year, by my last count."

In the silence that followed the confession of her dull existence, Biff pondered what it was in her nature that made her see things so clearly. Without question she had him pegged for a transient playboy who wouldn't know responsibility if it rose up and bit him. The mundane issues of day-to-day life were obviously beneath his notice.

He would have laughed if she hadn't been so serious. But while he didn't laugh, he didn't rush in, either, to put her out of her misery. She could just stew in her own pot for a few moments longer, he decided. If she was bent on proving they were incompatible, he might as well let her get it out of her system.

Then he could begin to prove just the opposite.

He reached into the bag and pulled out more bread, handing it to her without comment. His gaze wandered over her as she stared disconsolately down at the water, and he noticed the baggy sweats, the lack of makeup. Was this the worst she could do when she was really trying to look bad?

Amanda at her worst was more beautiful than most women at their best. She just didn't know it. He smiled to himself and silently acknowledged that his love for her might possibly color his judgment. No matter.

He cleared his throat. "Now that you've shown me your good side, what nasty surprises do you have in store for me?"

Her shoulders convulsed in an involuntary laugh. He pretended not to notice.

She looked at him, impatience heavy in her expression. "You just don't get it, do you?"

"Get what, darling? That you think I'm as useless as a flea when it comes to the everyday details of living? That I'm fickle, frivolous, and flighty?" He stared at her, his own impatience nudging at his mental balance.

He was torn between kissing her doubts away . . . and throwing her headfirst into the lagoon.

The lagoon was winning.

"That's not what this is about!" Jumping to her feet, she brushed the crumbs from her sweats. "I'm just trying to remind you that I don't belong in your world any more than you belong in mine."

He stood up beside her, blocking her escape just in case she intended to fight and run. "Given the assumption that you're out to lunch on both counts, why are you bringing this up now?"

Amanda looked at the man who was scowling at her and knew her heart wasn't in it. She could no more fight with Barley then she could kick a puppy.

She wanted to love him, even though she knew that she shouldn't. Bartholomew Fuller needed more out of life than peanut butter and bingo. He knew it. She knew it.

It was no good reminding him.

She was on her way to falling in love with him. And someday he would walk out of her life for good.

Biff was close enough to hear the great whoosh of air that she inhaled for courage. Fighting air, he imagined.

He couldn't have been more wrong.

Moving forward, she dropped her forehead onto his chest. "I'm sorry, Barley. I guess Mandy's Candies has left my nerves on edge."

He rested his forearms on her shoulders. "That's not why you picked a fight."

"I didn't mean to fight."

His fingers captured her chin and he raised her face to his. "You meant to put space between us, darling. As far as I'm concerned, that's fighting." He kissed her, a gentle touch that brought a sigh to her lips. "Promise me you'll not do that again?"

"Promise."

He kissed her once more, then hooked his fingers through hers and headed back to the condo. He'd come outside to tell her he loved her, and she had preempted him with doubts and worries. Now, though, he knew he couldn't tell her anything, not yet.

He loved her, but it wasn't enough.

She had to love him back . . . and that was a decision she had to make on her own.

Without undue influence.

EIGHT

Two days later Biff walked into the bedroom where Amanda was bent over double and rubbing her wet hair vigorously with a towel. She saw his feet first, bare beneath the jeans he seemed to prefer over almost anything else in his wardrobe.

She had counted six pairs of the stone-washed denims hanging in her closet alongside a couple of pairs of wool slacks, an assortment of shirts, two sport coats, and a dinner jacket with matching trousers. She'd vacated some of her precious drawer space for his use, and found a special thrill in seeing his personal things mixed with hers atop the dresser.

Amanda had never lived with a man, but never imagined it could be this easy. Where she'd expected an awkward adjustment as they got used to each other, there was a surprisingly balanced coexistence that made her wonder why she'd never tried it before.

Then again it was possible that with any other man it

wouldn't have been the same. Biff, she was beginning to believe, was the magic ingredient.

"Wyatt called while you were in the shower," he said, his hands brushing hers aside as he took over the task of drying her hair. "He has an appointment with Parks in a week."

"No kidding?"

"No kidding. Stand up now, darling. It's warm enough on the deck that you can let this dry in the sun."

She dropped the towel on the floor and flung her hair back from her face. "Is that all he said?"

"That's more or less it." He bent down to pick up the towel and took it into the bathroom. "Parks received the letter yesterday by express courier. Wyatt called him first thing this morning and set everything up." He pushed her lightly on the shoulder, picking up her brush as he urged her out toward the deck.

"Did he say how Anthony acted? Was he excited? Interested? Is it even worth it for Wyatt to come all this way?"

Biff laughed and pulled a chair around so that the morning sun fell directly on her wet hair. "Yes, he's excited. And interested. Wyatt wouldn't waste your money to fly over here if he thought differently."

He stood behind her and began to pull the brush through the tangles. It was one of his favorite jobs, one that Amanda seemed to enjoy equally. She slouched down in the chair and put her feet up on the small table opposite her, letting her head rest against the back of the chair. Her eyes closed in contentment, and the gleaming strands of her hair fell like silk around his fingers as he worked.

"Wyatt must owe you a pretty big favor to take time

off like this. Speaking of which, what *does* he do? You never mentioned it."

Because I didn't want to lie. Biff silently apologized to her and promised he'd tell her the whole truth as soon as it was practical. After she'd played out her own piece of the drama with Parks.

The less she knew, the greater chance she had of pulling it off.

"Biff?"

He cleared his throat and gave her the story he'd already cleared with Wyatt. "He manages an import-export business in Singapore. Don't worry about him losing time from work, though. Wyatt jumped at the chance to come stateside for a while."

"And the favor he owes you?"

She was like a puppy with a shoe, chewing and shaking it until all the interesting parts fell off. He threaded his fingers into her hair, sifting through its thickness to let the warm air dry it from within. "It happened a couple of years ago when I was researching a story on Java." He pulled over a bench and straddled it, then resumed working on her hair. "I was supposed to meet one of my sources at this dive down by the harbor. When I walked into the place, I found Wyatt with his back to the corner and a half-dozen local thugs real anxious to break a couple of bottles over his head."

"You knew him?" she asked.

"Not yet. We didn't get around to introducing ourselves until later."

She turned suddenly, folding her arms on the back of the chair and resting her chin on top of them, her eyes sparkling with fascination. "You saved Wyatt from getting creamed?"

He laughed and shook his head. "Probably not. I just helped even the odds. Wyatt can take care of himself without much help from anyone." He stroked the smooth backside of the brush across her cheek. "That's just how we met."

"And the favor?"

Persistent didn't begin to describe this woman he'd fallen in love with. "Wyatt was on Java looking for his sister, Elisabeth. She'd, er, gotten involved with a bad crowd, I guess you could say. One of the people I'd been talking to for my story was able to steer him in the right direction." He sidestepped the fact that it had been a kidnapping situation, because Wyatt had gone to great lengths to cover up the entire episode once he'd gotten his sister back. Perhaps someday Amanda would meet Elisabeth and hear the story firsthand. In the meantime it was a matter of respecting his friends' privacy.

He kissed Amanda on the mouth and stood up. "That's all, darling. Nothing very exciting. And like I said, Wyatt was dying for an excuse to come to San Francisco anyway."

She gave him a look that clearly meant she was reserving judgment, and turned around in her chair again, her drying hair a luscious fall of silk across the back of it. "Is there anyplace you haven't been, Barley?"

"As a matter of fact I've always wanted to see the Oregon coast." He moved to where she could see him. "What do you say we head up there tomorrow for a few days?"

"Just like that? Hop in the car and go sightseeing?" She sounded as though it was absurd even to consider it.

"It will have to be the truck," he said, smirking a little. "I wouldn't trust your car past the city limits—and that's a moot point anyway, considering the mechanic still has it."

"That's not what I meant," she retorted. "How can we just take off when so much is happening?"

"Why not? Wyatt won't be here until the day before his meeting with Parks, so there's nothing keeping us here that we can't do somewhere else." He waggled his brows in his very best imitation of a leer and bent over her chair until his face was inches from hers. "What do you say, darling? Shall we have a little vacation together?"

Her eyes darkened in a way that was fast becoming familiar to him. The onset of passion was a reality she'd never tried to hide from him. He wondered if she knew how rare that honesty was, how precious.

"What if Anthony changes his mind . . . or something happens and Wyatt needs to get hold of us?" she asked.

"Details," he said, brushing his lips across the bridge of her nose. "Leave them to me. You just go pack."

"Now?"

"Now. I have the urge to walk beside the ocean with you. Tonight."

"I don't think it's possible to get to Oregon before night," she murmured.

"Then the California coast will have to do." He found her hand and pulled her to her feet. "We'll take our time getting up north."

"What about reservations?"

"Details," he said again, his hand at the small of her back as he pushed her indoors. "And pack something that you can dance in, darling."

"We're going dancing?"

"We're going to do a lot of things, Amanda. Now, hurry up, please. I find myself anxious to get on our way."

He pulled a suitcase down from the top of her closet and opened it on the bed, waiting only until she started putting clothes into it before going into the other room to work on a few details.

He called Wyatt to let him know they'd check in with him from wherever they ended up that night. Just in case.

And he called the man he'd hired to keep an eye on Parks. Just in case.

It never hurt to cover all the bases.

They drove north along the coast highway, stopping for a late lunch at a little place just outside of Jenner before pressing on. Biff offered to let Amanda drive, but she declined, perfectly content to let him worry about the sometimes treacherous, winding road. Not that he worried, though. He handled the truck with the same easy control he did everything else.

It occurred to her that he handled her in pretty much the same way, gentle nudges when he wanted her to do one thing, delicate hints when he wanted her to do another. If she dug in her heels because she wanted something entirely different, he just smiled and let her think she was getting her own way.

She knew better. Nothing happened in Biff's world that wasn't by his design. She stared out the window at the fern-covered slope that flashed by in a kaleidoscopic blur and smiled. It wasn't a bad thing, this loss of control that she felt around him. In fact she'd never felt more secure in her entire life. What he wanted just happened to be what she wanted too.

It was something she'd miss when he was gone, this sense of well-being that was so different from what had passed for security before. How could a man who was so very much her opposite in goals and dreams bring her to this point? she wondered, sliding a glance in his direction.

He must have felt her stare, because he met her gaze and smiled. "You look sleepy."

She shook her head. "Just thinking."

His brows raised questioningly. "Not worried about Parks, are you?"

"No." Shifting until her shoulders were wedged against the door, she studied him with the unselfconscious curiosity that was reserved for people who had already shared the ultimate in intimacies. "I'm trying to figure out why I don't feel manipulated."

"What do you mean?" The look he shot her was interested rather than concerned. That pleased her, because it confirmed her suspicion that he didn't realize how thoroughly he was in control.

"I mean that ever since I met you, I've been following your lead without so much as a second thought."

"On the contrary," he said reasonably. "You had second and third thoughts the day I followed you into Blayne's office. It was touch and go for a minute there whether you were going to have him throw me out."

"But that's exactly my point. I bought into that little act of yours without so much as a whimper of protest." She bit down on her lip, both accepting and confused. "I'm doing things that are totally out of character. It worries me."

"Like what?"

"Like letting you move in with me."

"I thought it was what you wanted," he said, a frown creasing his forehead.

"It was." She laughed shortly, not surprised that she

was making a muddle out of explaining her conflicting emotions. "It's just that I've never done it before. And I really didn't even know you then."

"I disagree." His hand reached out for hers, enveloping it in the reassuring warmth of his touch. He tugged lightly, drawing her away from the door and closer to him. "You knew me well enough to make love with me that afternoon. Moving in with you was just a natural progression of events."

"Maybe in your world."

He glanced at her sharply, then turned his attention back to the road. "It has nothing to do with my world versus yours, darling. It might surprise you to know I've never done this before either."

He was right. She was surprised. "You've never lived with a woman?"

He shrugged. "It never seemed . . . appropriate." Keeping her hand in his, he downshifted and steered the truck through a sharp corner. "What else is out of character?"

"This trip is a good example. I never do anything on the spur of the moment. It isn't like me, but I was packed and out the door before I had a chance to think twice about it."

"You're not having fun?" he asked, his face relaxing into a smile.

"That's not the point." She crossed her legs Indian style on the bucket seat and sighed. "It's just that I've never simply locked the door and taken off . . . not without plans. It feels irresponsible."

There was a long silence as the truck wound its way down a steep hillside until they were once again skirting the ocean.

"Did you ever think," Biff asked, "that you've never done it before because you've never had the chance?" He relaxed against the leather seat and focused on a point somewhere up the road. "All those years you were building up Mandy's Candies can't have left you much time for goofing off. I'd imagine that whatever time you did find to get away had to be pretty well planned out."

She blinked at the simplicity of his reply. "You're right."

He brought her hand to his mouth and kissed the knuckle of her thumb. "It's never been my intention to manipulate you," he said quietly.

"If I didn't believe that, I wouldn't be here." Her hair fell over her face as she stared down at their joined hands, and she hid her smile behind it.

"It's true that I have a tendency to take charge of things," he said as if she hadn't spoken, "but I never meant for you to feel like you weren't in control."

She laughed under her breath. "I told you that I don't feel manipulated," she said firmly. "Out of control, yes. Manipulated, definitely not."

"Glad to hear it." A harsh breath whistled between his teeth, a clue that he was less than amused by her response.

Still, she couldn't resist teasing. "You're glad that I'm out of control?"

He didn't answer, not right away. A moment later he'd found a place to pull off the road and was parked before she had a chance to ask what he was about. Stomping down on the parking brake, he flipped a lever and pushed his seat as far back as it would go. Then he turned to her and clamped his hands around her arms.

He had her attention.

"Don't talk about control like it's something that I

must have just because you've lost it," he said, pulling her across the console until she was half-sitting, half-lying across his lap. His fingers stole into her hair and pressed her head against his chest.

She could hear the pounding of his heart beneath her ear, a rough cadence that underlined the tension in his body. When she tried to straighten so that she could look into his face, he stopped her. When she tried to speak, his thumb pressed her lips closed.

She waited.

"I followed you from Tahoe because I had to. There wasn't any decision making, just the knowledge that I had to be with you. Does that sound like a man in control of himself?" He stroked her hair and continued before she could reply. "I turned down an assignment for an article because it would have taken me to New Orleans next month, and I was afraid you wouldn't let me come back if I left you."

Nonsense, she thought. How could he think such a thing? Of course she'd let him come back . . . if he wanted to.

She'd known he was going to leave from the beginning. It had never occurred to her that he might come back.

"How long?" she whispered.

"The assignment?" His shoulders moved against her, and he answered distractedly. "A week or so, I guess. I wasn't willing to take the chance."

"I didn't know."

"I didn't tell you."

"I never asked you to give up anything—"

He interrupted with a hard shake of his head. "That's not what I meant. The assignment doesn't matter. What's important is you and me and what's happening to us."

"I remember now," she said, rubbing her cheek against his chest. "You said it that night in the casino . . . that something was happening to us, not between us. I thought it was a unique proposition."

"No, you didn't."

He shifted her in his arms until her mouth was beneath his. Her eyes drifted closed, and he kissed her with lingering sweetness, a tender expression of caring that made her heart swell with something she couldn't quite identify. She was floating in a dreamworld that began and ended with Barley, a fantasy that filled her with the incredible feeling of being exactly where she belonged.

He touched her lashes with his lips and murmured, "You knew exactly what I meant because you felt it too."

She shivered under the impact of what he was saying. It was more than a matter of being attracted to him, more than suddenly having a live-in lover.

More than she was ready to admit.

"I lost control," he said, kissing her face between words, "that very first moment in the casino when you looked at me and made me want you like I've never wanted another woman. Don't expect me to feel anything but relief if you're experiencing similar difficulties."

She giggled nervously and rubbed her nose against his chin. "You make it sound like a technical glitch."

His teeth fastened on her bottom lip in reprisal. She ran her tongue across his lips until he let go and sucked gently where he'd bitten her. They teased and parried that way until Amanda accidentally rolled against the gear shift, triggering the realization that there were, after all, better places for what they were doing. Setting her aside with only a heartfelt moan of regret, Biff started the truck and pulled back onto the road.

"So what you're telling me," she said, "is we're both out of control, and there's absolutely nothing we can do about it." She rested her hand on his thigh because she couldn't stand not touching him.

"It certainly looks that way to me." He put his hand on top of hers and squeezed. "I guess that whatever happened to us in Tahoe is running the show now, darling. The best we can do is to hold on tight and not let go."

They found a hotel just south of the Oregon border, a large resort-type establishment that was bordered by the ocean on one side and a golf course on the other. Amanda waited in the truck while he checked them in, her gaze fixed on the gray waters of the Pacific and her mind filled to overflowing with thoughts of Barley.

He was her lover, this man she'd known only a matter of days. He'd settled into her life with an ease that might have raised warning signals in her had she not understood him better.

She did understand him, though. She knew enough about Barley to realize it wasn't a case of his being used to moving around and therefore in the habit of adapting with very little fuss.

It was because he belonged with her. That was why everything was so easy between them.

He belonged with her.

Bartholomew Fuller, journalist-at-large, wandering the globe in search of the things that piqued his professional interest, was her lover. For a time.

She loved him, this man who would never stay in one place long enough to grow roots. The falling was over.

It wasn't something she'd known last night or even at lunchtime. The realization had come upon her as she'd watched him drive the lonely coast road toward a place he'd never been. He would smile at her, hold her hand, tease her with unrelenting persistence because she couldn't help but blush when he spoke of intimacies between them, both past and future.

He'd been patient with her questions about his life and vague about the answers. Barley was a private man, not taken to bragging or telling stories for effect. The things he had done were nothing less than adventures, it seemed to her, and his enthusiasm was boundless. He wanted to see everything, experience all that life had to offer.

Envy ripped through her, followed by an almost overwhelming sense of confusion. *Why should she envy him for doing the things she'd never had the slightest inclination to try?*

Nothing, it seemed, made much sense anymore.

Nothing, except for the fact that her heart was responding to Barley with an honesty she found impossible to ignore.

The sun had been setting in a slash of purple when he'd pulled into the hotel. She'd feigned weariness so that she could spend a few minutes alone and pull herself together. The heady acknowledgment of her love was tempered by sadness—and she didn't think she could dare to share either with him. Loving Barley was a mistake in the same way that a squirrel played too hard in the summer and found itself without food when the snow began to fall. The consequences were inevitable.

They belonged together now, but not tomorrow.

Because she loved him, she wanted her summer.

Because she loved him, she knew that the snow would come.

The tide rushed in, waves breaking over each other in their eagerness to reach the sand. Amanda chewed on her thumbnail and wondered how much she should tell him . . . and worried about how much he already knew.

NINE

Their suite had an ocean view and a fireplace that was built into the wall between the bedroom and living room. Biff dumped their bags inside, then pulled Amanda along with him for what he said would have to be a quick walk. The light was nearly gone, but there was still time if they hurried.

It was cold and windy down by the water, and in the end they stayed much longer than was really sensible.

They couldn't help it. The draw of the ocean was more powerful than either could resist. They walked at the edge of the foaming waves, holding hands, dividing their attention between each other and the ocean.

The emotional turmoil of the afternoon mellowed inside of Amanda as she took deep, cleansing breaths of the salt air. Being with Biff was as close to heaven as she'd ever been.

She knew she had no choice but to tell him, soon, before he guessed and things got unnecessarily complicated. Trying to pretend love hadn't happened was beyond her acting abilities. Simple role-playing was one thing, but major-league emotions were on the line here, and she knew better than to imagine she could bluff her way around them. Biff had the uncanny ability to know what she was thinking almost before she did herself.

Still, she imagined that telling him would be a lot like jumping off a cliff—where that first step into nothing was completely irrevocable.

Once said, the words of love could never be taken back.

Why did the prospect of taking that first step into midair sound so appealing?

His hand tugged at hers, and he pulled her to a stop on the hard sand. He cupped her face with cold fingers, gently forcing her to meet his gaze. "What's wrong, darling? You've been brooding about something for the last hour."

"Brooding?" She couldn't help but smile because he almost always guessed right the first time. "How do you know I'm not just tired?"

"Are you?"

She shook her head. "*Brooding* is probably as good a word as any."

"Anything you want to tell me about?" His lips brushed over her forehead in a light caress.

She shivered, and not from the cold. He put his arm around her shoulders anyway and steered her back in the direction of the hotel.

"Biff?"

"Hmm?"

"Would you mind very much if I told you that I was in love with you?"

His step faltered, as if there was something in his path that made him pause before continuing on. It was only a slight hesitation, barely noticeable, especially when he resumed their former pace without any detectable difficulty.

"You sound as if the thought of falling in love with me grieves you," he said, hugging her just the slightest bit closer to his side. "Is there a problem here that I don't know about?"

Typical Biff, she thought. Nothing fazed him. Not even love.

"That it grieves me would be an exaggeration," she said, her arm around his waist as they plowed through the deeper sands and high grasses over which the ocean rarely flowed. "I just mentioned it because it was something that occurred to me this afternoon. I thought you might like to know."

"Does it make any difference about how you want to go about things?" he asked.

She had to think about that one for a bit. Any difference? No, not really. Except for knowing that winter's solitude would surely follow the frolics of summer, there was nothing in the forecast that should affect anything.

"No difference," she said, leaning into his body as they stepped together over the low stone wall that bordered the hotel. Now that she'd said the words, she felt better. Much better.

Jumping off a cliff wasn't nearly as frightening as she'd imagined. With a determination founded in the joy that suddenly filled her, she quit thinking about what would happen when she hit bottom.

"I really do love you," she said into his silence, the trust she'd had for him from the beginning lending her the courage to be honest. "I guess I needed to tell you because . . ." She took a deep breath and tried again. "I needed to tell you because it wasn't something I wanted to hide."

"Good."

A single word that accepted what she'd said . . . and approved. She couldn't ask for more than that, not now.

They arrived at the door to their suite, and he put the key into the lock without letting go of her. Pulling her inside, he slammed the door shut and backed her against it, his hands braced against the door on either side of her head.

"Tell me again," he demanded, his face an indistinct blur in the dark hallway.

"I love you."

"You're sure?" he asked, his voice husky with emotion. He hadn't expected this from her, not this soon . . . not this openly. To say he'd been taken by surprise would have been an understatement.

"I'm sure."

He found her mouth in the darkness. She parted her lips beneath the pressure of his, inviting him inside, her tongue sliding across his with a delicacy that touched off an erotic response deep within him. He thrust inside her mouth, tasting her, enjoying her. His hands were buried in her hair, the silken waves capturing him as surely as her mouth enticed him into a kiss that was even deeper than before . . . better, if that were possible.

His lips slanted across hers in a quick, hard kiss, then he backed away, reaching to flip on the light. His eyes narrowed as he watched her from a safe distance, knowing that if he touched her again, the fire would consume them.

He wanted more.

He wanted her to know that their lovemaking was special because they were both in love. Not just her, but the two of them sharing something precious and rare.

She blinked at the sudden brightness, and he waited for her eyes to adjust before backing into the living room, his hand outstretched to urge her forward. "Come inside, darling," he said. "I think we have a couple of things to sort out."

Amanda knew what he was going to say. He was going to tell her that she shouldn't hope for forever, because he couldn't give it to her. They had here and now, not some distant future. Even tomorrow was a hope, not a promise.

She knew that.

The glare of the lights kept her from seeing the expression in his eyes, but she'd studied the next scene and was ready to play her part. It had been a risk, telling him, but risk taking was something she was learning from him.

Throwing her coat over a chair, she sank onto the sofa and watched as he fiddled with the gas igniter on the fireplace.

"We shouldn't light that if we're going to the dining room for dinner," she said.

"I haven't thought as far as dinner." He shut off the

gas and took a deep breath, his shoulders shifting beneath what appeared to be a bothersome strain. "I'm having trouble enough wondering how we're going to get through the next five minutes."

"Because we have to talk?"

He spun from the brick fireplace, his hands fisted at his sides. "Because I want to make love with you, dammit, and there's so much that needs to be said before we do."

Taking a deep breath for courage, she preempted the speech he appeared determined to make. "Promise me something, Barley?"

"What?"

"When you leave, don't forget to say good-bye."

"What do you mean, 'when I leave'? Have I said anything about leaving you?" he asked harshly.

"Not today." She uncurled her legs from beneath her and stood up, walking toward him without letting her gaze waver from the definitely menacing one he was leveling on her. "But you will. Next week or next month, when it's time for Bartholomew Fuller to get on with his business."

She reached him, laid her hands on his chest, and discovered that his heart was beating as fast as her own. "You'll leave me one day. When it's time for you to get on with your life." She lifted onto her toes and touched her lips to his cheek. "I love you, Barley. And if you don't say good-bye, I'll go crazy wondering when you're coming back."

"You sound like good-bye is forever."

"It should be, don't you think? Love affairs have to end sometime or other. Making a clean break has got to be easier than not knowing if it's really over."

"You seem to know a lot more about this than I do."

She shook her head. "Guesswork, that's all."

Biff looked down into her solemn gaze, holding a tight rein on the anger that burned his soul. She expected so little from him . . . so much less than he was prepared to give.

Cupping her face in his hands, he played the only card he had. "What if I told you that I love you too?"

Her eyes closed tight, just for a moment. When they fluttered open again, he discovered new depths to Amanda that he hadn't imagined existed.

"I would say, Barley, that this is one hell of a mess we've gotten ourselves into." She smiled, a tremulous offering that he found irresistibly endearing. "Wouldn't you agree?"

He bent his head to hers, their foreheads touching before he tilted her face so that he could feel her lips beneath his.

"Yes, darling," he said between hard, wet kisses. "This is one hell of a mess. Do you want to make love or go to dinner and talk it over?"

"Can't we do both?"

He smiled against her lips and murmured that they could do whatever she wished.

She made her wishes in order of importance.

It was late when they went to the main lodge for dinner, Biff in a pair of soft-wool slacks, linen shirt, tie, and sport coat, Amanda in a long-sleeved silk dress of sapphire blue. The skirt flared full and sassy just above her knees, and the bodice hugged her figure with breathtaking honesty. Definitely made for dancing, he'd said after fixing her zipper, his hands warming her shoulders that were exposed by the boat-cut neckline.

Following the maître d' to a table by the windows, Amanda felt Biff's gaze on the bare nape of her neck and shivered. He'd insisted that she wear her hair up, caught in a pair of golden combs he had bought for her earlier that afternoon during one of their many stops. She'd argued that she thought he preferred her to wear it down.

But taking it down is half the thrill, darling.

She slid into the chair Biff was holding for her and braced herself for the brush of his lips across her neck. He brushed, she shivered, and she heard his deep, satisfied chuckle as he took the chair opposite.

"You knew that was coming, darling," he said after giving the order for champagne—Taittinger, naturally. "Why the shivers?"

"Knowing and being able to do anything about it are entirely different things." She reached forward and moved the candle aside so that she could see his face without having to tilt her head. "You're perfectly aware that I've never been able to hide anything from you."

His gaze locked on her with feverish intensity. "Did you know how sexy I find your honesty?"

She blushed, then laughed because he'd done it again—made her react with so little effort. There was nothing he did that she was able to ignore, nothing that didn't elicit a tiny response.

She basked in his attention and gave him as much of herself as there was to give.

The waiter returned with the champagne, making an elegant presentation of the bottle before removing the cork with a delicate pop. The wine was poured, a silent toast was made between the lovers as the waiter tactfully turned away to fiddle with the ice bucket. It was a moment in time, much like that first night in Tahoe, their first bottle of champagne, then the silence was broken by a discreet cough. The waiter, they remembered, their eyes filling with shared laughter. They weren't alone, not yet. They discussed appetizers and entrées, but Amanda's mind was only partly involved with the decisions.

She was remembering the exquisite hours preceding dinner, that magical time in which she'd come to believe that Barley, her lover, was also in love.

With her.

And they said miracles never happened! A huge sigh of happiness welled up inside her. He'd convinced her first with words, then had gone on to emphasize the point with kisses and caresses. Their lovemaking had been at once tender and frantic, the urgency of their passion tempered by the awareness that they'd never done it before . . . not quite that way, not with love.

She remembered his statement of when it had happened, and where. Love, he'd insisted, had happened to them in Tahoe. And love had brought them back together again.

The waiter melted away, making his own decisions on what they would eat, since he hadn't received much help from either of the people at the table. Amanda smiled over the top of her glass, catching Biff's equally amused glance with hers.

"You can't expect me to believe that it was love at first sight," she said, sipping her champagne. "Things like that only happen in the movies."

"Just because you're slow to catch on doesn't mean it didn't happen," he teased, his eyes twinkling with amusement.

"Three days is slow?"

"Three days can be a lifetime." His voice was a husky drawl that sent renewed shivers through her.

She took a deep breath and said, "So what are we going to do about this?"

"Nothing."

Her eyebrows rose in surprise. "Nothing?"

He nodded. "I think we've got enough to worry about now with Mandy's Candies and Parks. Why don't we get through that before we, er, refocus our attention?"

She agreed eagerly. It suited her to agree, because putting it off was better than facing facts. Facts such as knowing they were totally unsuited to each other.

"My grandfather once told me," he went on, "that it was better to sit back and let a problem solve itself rather than to impose a half-assed solution that probably wouldn't work anyway."

She giggled. "I think I would have liked your grandfather."

"He would have liked you too."

She was going to ask more about the man Barley so admired, when the waiter arrived with appetizers that smelled like garlic and looked like something that slithered out of a shell. He fussed for a moment, then disappeared.

"Escargot?" she asked, wrinkling her nose in exaggerated distaste. "I don't remember ordering this."

Biff laughed. "This is what you get for not paying attention. Why don't you try it before you turn up your nose?"

Never in a million years, she thought, appalled as he forked one of the slugs onto a piece of toast and slid it into his mouth. "Ugh!" she said, a shiver of a different kind threatening her composure.

He ate another one, lifting a brow at her squeamishness. "And here I thought you were a sophisticated lady."

"I told you I was peanut butter," she muttered, picking up a piece of toast and chewing on it.

He shook his head in mild reproof. "Don't start that again, darling. I happen to know better."

She shrugged, thinking that peanut butter would go a heck of a lot better with champagne than the slimy things he was eating.

"So what have you got against snails?"

"Only a memory that goes back to when I was about eight and little Shawn Parker made me eat one before he'd let me into his treehouse." She shuddered again, the memory still vivid after all these years. "To this day I won't eat the things, no matter how nicely disguised they are."

"You want me to get you something else?"

"That depends on what I ordered for dinner."

"I think it was salmon of some sort," he said, reaching across the table to appropriate her escargot. "Will that do?"

"As long as it isn't cooked in 'paste d' escargot,' or something equally repulsive."

"I think you're safe." Without appearing to hurry, he quickly finished the remaining escargot so that she wouldn't have to watch any longer than necessary.

"Tell me about your parents," she said when the waiter had cleared the offensive plates away. "I'll bet they weren't too happy with your decision not to join the family business. It must worry them, all this traveling that you do."

He laughed, a genuinely amused sound that crinkled his eyes and softened the harsh lines of his face. "I always figured my dad was more envious of my lifestyle than he was mad that I wouldn't join him. As it was, he ran the company for exactly ten years after Grandfather died before selling out."

"That's all?"

He nodded. "My folks decided they wanted to see the world before they were too old to enjoy it. Thanks to Grandfather and the business, they can afford to do it." Biff decided not to mention that his grandfather had left him with his own safety net in the form of a sizable trust fund. It was going to be hard enough convincing Amanda that his career and all the traveling that went with it wasn't a threat to her perception of security. To have her worry that he could quit whenever he wished would only complicate things that were already . . . complicated.

Security wasn't a financial condition, so his trust fund was essentially irrelevant. Besides, he had other plans for the money that didn't include more than a token amount being set aside for his own use. He was well enough off, thanks to his own career, and there were so many people who had nothing. Next year, when the bulk of the trust became available, he intended to set up a foundation that would make better use of Grandfather's gift.

No, security wasn't a financial condition. Nor was it a place. It was a state of mind, of heart.

He wasn't sure how to go about persuading Amanda of that.

"Where do your parents live?" she asked.

"London, for the most part, although I'd bet almost anything that they haven't spent more than two or three weeks there in the last year. They like to get around."

What with their going yachting in Australia, orchid hunting up the Amazon, and ghost busting in Ireland, Biff had trouble finding them with any sort of predictability.

"So that's where you get it from," she said with what he could have sworn was a look of sheer envy on her face.

"Get what from?"

"The wanderlust."

TEN

She had it, too, and didn't know it. Wanderlust.

Biff lowered his gaze, hiding the satisfaction he felt. He'd sensed it in her before, but her denials had thrown him off. Amanda, though, would have to come to her own conclusions for them to hold any weight with her.

That didn't mean he couldn't give her the occasional shove in the right direction.

They ate dinner quickly, eager to retire to the lounge, where other couples were slow-dancing to soft music. When he led her to the edge of the dance floor, he found pleasure in taking it one step at a time. First he slipped his arm around her waist. Holding her gaze steadily with his, he took her right hand and folded it within his much larger one. With a firm tug he pulled her forward until her head nested under his chin, their joined hands tucked against his heart. The hand at her back pressed her closer, and only then did he begin to move.

Amanda felt herself being drawn across the floor in a

steady, shuffling rhythm that was so restful, she forgot to worry about little things like stepping on his foot or going left when he was heading right. It was as though they'd danced together before, the steps an unconscious duplication of something they'd learned and practiced until they'd gotten it just right.

Her hand crept up his shoulder to his neck, her fingers threading into his hair. She heard his soft groan of approval as she toyed with it and knew her own pleasure as the silky strands tangled in her hand.

He pulled her closer, his lips buried in her hair as he guided her across the floor. When the music changed, one slow song replacing another, he whispered that he loved her and continued their dance.

She knew it was crazy to dream, but she did it anyway. She couldn't help it—the night, the music, his arms around her in an embrace so tender and protective that she felt more secure than she'd ever felt in her life. He loved her, she loved him. Their love had strength, she imagined, a magic that made anything possible. All she needed was Barley. The rest didn't matter, nothing was as important as being with him. They could build their dream together, show the world that two people who loved each other could do the impossible.

It was crazy to dream, but she was too caught up in it to have the will to do anything else. Tonight she was with the man she loved, and nothing on earth could take away the joy of being loved in return.

They danced for hours, until the clock passed midnight and everyone else had long since gone. He bundled her into her coat for the cold, windy trip back to their suite, but she felt only the heat of wanting him as he hustled her across the courtyard.

He busied himself with the fire as she slipped out of her shoes and struggled with the zipper at the back of her dress. She was no longer shy around him, but was instead filled with the need to be with him as intimately as a woman could be with a man.

He pulled a sheet from the bed and stretched it out on the floor in front of the fire, then stripped off his own clothes before helping her finish taking off hers.

They stood naked before the fire, touching without holding, pausing for a moment before the impending storm of passion consumed them.

"I love you, Barley Fuller," she told him, and smiled when he kissed her on the forehead and asked her to say it again.

She did, and felt an exciting shiver of joy as his low, rough voice repeated the words back to her.

"Darling?"

She looked up into his dark, heated stare. "Hmm?"

"Do you think you could do me a favor?" he asked, his hands resting lightly at her hips.

She put her own hands on his chest and felt the power of his heart thudding within. "Of course."

"You don't even know what it is." He chuckled, a husky rumble that she felt beneath her hands. "You shouldn't be taking chances like that."

"Why not?" She touched her lips to his chest, trailing light kisses until she found an erect nipple with her tongue.

He groaned, but didn't move to stop her. "Because you don't know that I won't take advantage of you."

She grinned against his chest. "Take advantage of me, Barley. *Please* take advantage of me."

Biff tightened his hands at her hips as he resisted

succumbing to the humor in her voice. He pulled her tight against his aroused body. "The favor, Amanda. It's important." He knew his voice had a strangled undertone to it, but that was only because it was nearly impossible to talk when she was doing crazy things to him with her tongue.

"What kind of a favor?" she asked. She wasn't really interested, though, because there were other things she wanted to do that didn't include talking. Sliding down his body, she rediscovered him with her hands—rock-hard thighs covered with dark, springy hair. The satiny strength of his manhood. On her knees, she followed her hands with her mouth—and reveled in his uninhibited, shuddering reaction as she discovered the excitement of pleasing him in yet another way. His hips rocked convulsively, and she thought she heard him beg her to stop.

She didn't even consider it. She managed to ignore his protests until he dug his fingers into her hair and forced her back to her feet.

"It wasn't that kind of favor," he said harshly, dragging her against him.

"No?" Her arms lifted to twine around his neck, her body adjusting to his as he pulled her even closer.

"Darling—"

She rubbed against him in a move that was so sensually exciting, he lost his ability to speak.

"Barley, what do you say we talk about it later, hmm?"

He groaned and buried his face in her hair. "You win, darling. We'll talk later."

He took his defeat like a man . . . a man in love. In front of a fire that was an insubstantial reflection of the flames that burned between them, he made long, slow love to Amanda.

He murmured words of love and promises of forever, not imagining that she could distinguish one from the other.

She must have, though, because she matched him promise for promise as they rode their passion to its explosive peak, and those promises quite literally took his breath away.

It had been a dream.

Amanda awakened with the first light of dawn, curled up beside Barley on the bed they'd somehow managed to reach not so many hours earlier. It came back to her with outrageous clarity, the things he'd said at the height of passion . . . words that had sounded suspiciously like *always* and *forever*.

It had been a dream. It couldn't be anything else. She edged away from the sleeping man and tiptoed to the bathroom, pushing the door closed and leaning against it as she released a panicked sigh.

She'd heard what she wanted to hear, she told herself. Promises. Vows. Pledges of a life spent together—an absurd notion because they both knew it would never work. He was a traveler. She wasn't.

A dream. She took a deep breath and turned on the water for a shower. A ridiculous dream, she repeated, waiting as the water heated before stepping inside. She lifted her face to the stinging spray, aware that the dream was no less vivid now than it had been upon waking.

Just a dream. Barley had made promises, and she'd

said things in return, words of love that were wrapped in the concept of forever.

It had felt so real.

"You're up early."

The noise of the shower had kept her from hearing him come into the bathroom. She wiped her eyes, opened them, and saw Barley leaning against the edge of the shower—not quite in but not on the other side of the curtain either.

"I couldn't sleep." She grabbed the bottle of shampoo, pouring a dab into her palm and trying hard to act as though she wasn't the least bit disturbed by this man who watched her with such casual familiarity. Her heart was thudding in her chest, but, of course, he would know that.

Barley knew everything.

He made no move to join her, just held the shower curtain aside enough to let them talk without getting water all over the floor. She massaged the shampoo into her hair and waited to see what he'd do next.

"We never got back to that favor I was asking you about last night."

She grinned. "You do pick the oddest moments for discussion."

"It's important, darling," he said, his voice a low rumble that cut through the noise of the running water. "I need you to promise me something."

Promise. Her blood pounded in her ears as she remembered the last time she'd used that word. "Seems like you owe me one first."

He looked confused, and she said with a small laugh, "Yesterday I asked you to promise me you'd say good-bye."

"I'd forgotten that," he said, frowning as he rested a

shoulder against the tile wall. "But I guess it's all to do with the same thing. I still want your promise."

She stopped washing her hair and stepped back from the spray. He was serious. Serious, and quite determined to talk.

"I'll promise you anything, Barley," she said softly. "You know that."

"Then promise you won't write me off before you give us a chance."

So that was it. She met his earnest gaze and felt as though the world was spinning faster than before. "I thought we weren't going to worry about this at all until Mandy's Candies is sorted out."

He shook his head. "That's not good enough anymore," he said. "Last night changed everything. You have to know that."

"It was a dream," she said, suddenly frightened by something she couldn't define.

"No, Amanda. It wasn't." A half smile curved his lips. "We both said things that we wanted to say. I just don't want you to forget them."

"You know it won't work," she said, swallowing over the sadness that welled in her throat. "It can't."

"That's what I want you to promise, darling." He reached forward to stroke her wet cheek with his thumb. Not tears, she hoped. Just the shower. "Don't put an end to whatever it is that we have together before we've hardly begun."

"You were going to ask me last night," she said slowly as she remembered the sequence of events. "You asked me for the favor before we made love . . . before we said all those things."

He grinned sheepishly. "I knew what I was going to

say long before we finished dancing." His fingers left her cheek to trace a line across her shoulder. "The only surprise was when you agreed."

"What did I agree to?" But she knew, and her heart was pounding so hard that she could barely hear what he said in reply.

"Forever." The fingers of his other hand curled around the curtain rod, the knuckles turning white from his fierce grasp. "Promise me, darling, that you won't take it back without giving us a chance." He waited, his smile a faded memory, the shower a pounding rhythm in the otherwise soundless room.

"I promise." She shrugged in helpless compliance. "I can't seem to say no to you."

"It's okay, then." His gaze swept over her, hot and victorious.

Her stomach turned somersaults, and she hid her reaction by ducking under the spray to rinse her hair. Even with her eyes closed she knew he was still there. She lifted her arms to run her fingers through her soapy hair and squealed in surprise when she felt him touch the tender spot under her arm. She dropped her arms in a rush and stepped out of the spray.

"Tell me about the scar, darling," he said when she'd wiped the water from her eyes.

The scar. She hadn't thought about it in years. Not that she had much reason to, of course, given that it was located in her armpit and she was rarely in a position to catch a glimpse of it.

She grinned and stared pointedly at the inch-long scar on his face. "Not unless you tell me first."

"Now I know why you never asked about it," he

drawled, tracing his scar with a long finger. "You had your own embarrassing story to hide."

"Not too embarrassing actually." She edged back toward the streaming water. "Stupid, yes. But I was young and didn't embarrass very easily. How about you?"

"I was twenty-something."

"And?" she prodded.

"Does a parrot on Bali give you a clue?"

She laughed and wished she had something equally as silly to relate. But she didn't. "I was seven, and Billy Larkin dared me to climb the garage roof." She shrugged. "I climbed. I fell. Unfortunately it was onto a stack of boards that had nails sticking out every which way."

He winced. "I think I preferred the parrot."

She agreed, but when she opened her mouth to tell him, he'd already tugged the shower curtain closed and was gone.

Amanda was alone, with only her thoughts to keep her company. She took a deep breath and ducked her head back under the rushing stream.

Forever.

She wondered if she would ever have the courage and the strength to make it happen.

They left after lunch and spent the afternoon exploring the ragged beauty of the Oregon coast. The hotel they found wasn't as luxurious as the one where they'd stayed the first night, but neither cared. It was clean and private, and the dining room provided a more down-home version of the fresh fish they both thoroughly enjoyed.

They spent the next few days wandering up and down the coast, sometimes venturing inland to experience the almost claustrophobic feeling that came from being enveloped by the seemingly unending forests of fir and pine trees. Dozens of shades of green cascaded across hillsides and valleys, almost to the exclusion of all the other colors of nature's original rainbow. It reminded him of Ireland, he said. Not the trees so much as the variety of green.

He told her about kissing the Blarney stone and taking a pony-drawn cart up to the exact place where Saint Patrick had killed the last snake in Ireland. She asked about the article he'd written while he was there and vicariously met the people who had shared their stories with him, stories he'd retold for the world to read.

He made her want to see the things he'd seen. Perhaps she'd take a vacation, she thought, but there was a niggling suspicion deep inside that hearing his stories firsthand was much more exciting than making the trip herself . . . *by* herself.

They roamed the countryside for hours at a time, but it was the ocean that drew them time and again, their mutual affinity for boulder-strewn beaches a bond they accepted without remarking on it.

One afternoon Biff pulled a lap-top computer from the back of the truck, and they sat down to work out the "proposal" from Paradise Hotels. Actually Amanda mostly watched as Biff typed legal-sounding sentences until there were nearly three pages of offers, promises, requirements, and figures. It amazed her how easily he was able to make it look and sound legitimate, and she told him so. He just laughed and said that being a writer had its advantages.

They faxed the finished copy to Wyatt so that he could transfer it to the expropriated stationery. Biff repacked the computer into the truck and took her to a movie. They held hands and shared a giant box of popcorn amid a crowd comprised of parents and toddlers, the film being an animated adventure story that Biff swore was geared to the adult mentality.

She didn't care what was on the screen as long as they were watching it together.

Over the next couple of days they rehearsed her upcoming scene with Anthony, going over her lines one by one. It wasn't that he expected her to use his exact words, Biff told her, but with a script she wouldn't have to make up anything on the spot. He was concerned that without a script she'd let her emotions get in the way and say things that would blow the entire con sky high.

All she had to do was convince Anthony that Blayne had turned up information that Wyatt and Paradise were linked to drug trafficking. It would be up to Anthony to decide if that was a good thing or bad thing. Based on everything Amanda had told Biff about Anthony, he wasn't concerned that Parks would pursue the opportunity once he had all the "facts." If Parks had wanted to get into the drug trade, he would certainly have done so long before now.

Parks was greedy, Biff said. Greedy, not stupid. That was why they had to time everything so tight. Given more than a few hours to think about it, Parks might do his own investigation and discover the lies within Amanda's story.

And so they rehearsed. By the time they arrived back in the Bay Area almost a week later, Amanda was confident she could carry it off. She was excited and nervous and so on edge, Biff made her soak in the tub for an entire hour before he let her come to bed that night. After a long drive, he told her, he could do without all that nervous energy in bed with them.

When he finally pulled her from the bath, he was satisfied to find that her nerves had settled beneath soft, flushed skin that was extra-sensitive to his touch. He took charge of drying her with a fluffy towel, finding particular interest in how she reacted when he stroked the backs of her knees and thighs. He told her she felt like warm satin all over, then made her lie down on the bed as he massaged lotion over every inch of her body. Satin was something that needed care, he murmured, and delighted in the task, which wasn't really work at all.

They made slow, luxurious love that night, and by the time Biff finally closed his eyes, Amanda was already sound asleep in his arms. It felt good to be home, he thought as he tucked the comforter around them.

When Amanda met Wyatt, she found herself thinking that he looked like a man who had serious underworld connections. He was tall and powerfully built, and there was a leashed strength about him that his well-tailored clothes couldn't hide. His skin and hair were darker than Barley's, his eyes a color of gray that reminded her of cold steel. All in all he radiated a certain menace that was almost tangible.

As far as first impressions went, she was pretty well intimidated. That was until he smiled, a flicker of something that resembled approval as Barley murmured introductions and pulled her forward. The smile was gone almost before she noticed it, but she was certain she'd seen it.

She liked him immediately.

They met in downtown San Francisco at the luxury hotel Wyatt had booked himself into the night before.

When she'd heard where he was staying, she had worried that her designated expense money—four and a half thousand dollars—wouldn't last the week. Barley had told her not to worry because Wyatt knew someone who knew someone, and his room was cheap, if not free.

It seemed like she'd heard that story before. Barley was always explaining things away that way. She'd shrugged and decided that whatever the cost, it would be worth it. Even if they went over budget.

They went to one of the hotel's restaurants for lunch. Seated in the booth between the two men, Amanda ordered a salad and listened carefully as Wyatt and Barley went over the details of the con.

"Have you called Parks yet?" Barley asked.

"Last night, just to let him know I'm here and to confirm our meeting tomorrow. I didn't give him a chance to go into the details." Wyatt took a long drink of his soda water, then poured some more into the glass. "Jet lag," he said apologetically before taking another swallow.

"Do you have the proposal with you?" Barley asked, his hand finding Amanda's in her lap and pulling it onto his thigh.

"The papers are all upstairs. We can go up after lunch and I'll give you a copy." He paused as the waiter dropped off bread and butter. "I made a couple of changes before transferring the proposal to the Paradise letterhead, but they were only minor."

"Always glad to have a second opinion."

Wyatt looked at him and said, "Your grandfather would have been proud."

"Raw talent," Barley said with conspicuous modesty. "Seriously, Wyatt, I'd go nuts if I had to sit in an office and do stuff like that every day like you do."

"You think it's easy for me?" Wyatt asked, shaking his head as he turned to Amanda. "Now, Amanda, why don't you tell me everything there is to know about Mandy's Candies. I need to have as much information as Parks does if I'm going to be convincing."

"I thought Barley already filled you in," she said, taking her hand back when she saw Wyatt's gaze stray in that direction. It was a business lunch, she reminded herself. Holding hands was definitely not appropriate.

"Barley?" Wyatt's eyebrows raised a quarter inch, and he flashed one of his rare smiles in Biff's direction. "The last person I heard call you that nursed a broken jaw for six weeks."

Amanda shot him a look of disbelief being turning back to Wyatt. "He introduced himself as Barley first. It never occurred to me . . ." Her words trailed off as she tried to remember that it wasn't polite to laugh at a person's name. Barley had been tough enough, although she had to admit that she was quite attached to it now. Biff, on the other hand, was a name that always raised a giggle or a snicker deep inside.

She giggled. *And* snickered. She couldn't help it. "I always thought Barley was infinitely preferable to Biff," she said, clenching her teeth in an attempt to stifle any further laughter. It didn't work at all well. "Now, if you'd told me he slugged someone who called him Biff . . ."

"It was the *way* he said it," Barley protested. "I don't much care what people call me as long as they say it nicely."

"So I guess laughing is out," Amanda said, trying valiantly to get her own giggles under control. It was difficult. Now that the cat was out of the bag, so to speak, she felt like it was open season on "Biff."

He shot her a look that was meant to quell her and muttered something vaguely obscene under his breath. Then he told her to get on with it. The thing about Mandy's Candies.

It took a gallant effort, but she managed to smother most of the laughter, letting out only a couple of stray chortles as she began to tell Wyatt about how Anthony had weaseled her business away from her. Wyatt interrupted almost before she'd begun and told her to go back to the very beginning, when she'd first started the company.

Though she didn't understand why he needed such detail, she complied. Over lunch she talked, answered questions, and filled in the gaps when he noticed even the tiniest of lapses. It took nearly two hours, after which she was drained of anything that resembled energy. The two men left her at the table, Wyatt saying he was looking forward to having dinner with the two of them after his meeting with Parks the next day. Barley went along with him to get the proposal, a trip Amanda couldn't bring herself to make.

She sipped coffee and wondered what it was about the last hours that had felt less like an information-gathering session than an in-depth interview. She sighed and knew that whatever reason, she felt as though she'd been put through the wringer.

Barley was back in just minutes. He helped her to her feet, slipped an arm around her waist, and assured her they'd be home in no time.

"I felt better after working twenty-hour days when I first started Mandy's Candies," she complained as they sped north across the Golden Gate Bridge. "What is it about that guy that makes you feel you've been sucked dry by a vampire?"

Biff grinned and patted her hand. "He's just a little intense, that's all. Don't let it bother you, darling. He affects everybody that way."

"You don't seem any worse for wear." She groaned and wondered how she'd ever get out of the truck with jelly for legs. Oh, well, she'd just have to depend on Barley. Biff. She giggled.

"I wasn't under the microscope," he said logically, slanting a look at her that meant he'd heard the giggle and was putting it down to fatigue. "Trust me, Amanda. I've been there and I know how you feel."

"Yeah, right," she muttered, slouching deeper into the seat. "You wouldn't know jelly if it jumped up and bit you."

"Jelly?"

She nodded. It was the last thing she remembered before falling asleep.

ELEVEN

The first thing Amanda did the next morning was to call her mechanic and ask very politely why it had been over a week now and she hadn't heard from him about the Hillman.

Her Husky, as he preferred to call it, was almost fixed. Another day or two and he'd have it ready. And no, it wasn't going to cost a fortune. Then he told her how much.

Money, she realized, was relative. Obviously a mechanic specializing in foreign cars was several income categories above her.

She hung up, convinced he was keeping the car to impress the girl she'd seen hanging around the garage the last couple of times she'd been in. It never occurred to her that the Hillman wasn't exactly "girlfriend-impressing" material.

"What time is Wyatt's meeting?" she asked Barley.

He looked up from the newspaper he was reading and

shook his head in mild reproof. "I've answered that question three times this morning, Amanda. Do you think you can actually listen when I tell you this time?"

She had the grace to blush. "It's just that I'm a little nervous."

"The meeting is at eleven," he said gently. "Wyatt will call as soon as he can."

"Do you think—"

He cut her off before she could get started on yet another version of the "what ifs." "I think that Wyatt will call at the first opportunity, and all we can do is hang around here and wait."

Amanda scowled as he returned his attention to the paper. Easy for him to say. It wasn't his life that was being gambled away. Muttering under her breath, she went out to the deck and leaned on the railing, staring blindly at the lagoon below.

She didn't hear his approach, but she sensed it. Barley was behind her, standing silent and calm and so damned assured that she was ready to slug him.

She turned and walked into his open arms, burying her face against his chest. "I'm sorry, Barley," she said. "It's just that it's the first time since I started Mandy's Candies that I've let anyone else be in control."

"You're still in control, darling," he said, stroking her hair with a steady, even touch. "It just doesn't feel like it because you're not there in person to pin Parks to the wall."

"Pins sound good," she said. "Maybe I could find an old picture . . ."

He chuckled and pulled her closer. "Just remember that you'll have your chance. Escrow is due to close Friday. Today is Monday. If Parks takes the bait, Wyatt will force him to sign on Thursday or the deal is off. You'll go into your act shortly thereafter. By Friday morning this will all be history."

"Exactly how much of this did you tell Blayne?" she asked. Barley had called her attorney the night before while she slept off Wyatt's interrogation.

"Enough." He backed into a chair and pulled her onto his lap, never once stopping the comforting strokes that were lulling her into a sense of relaxed security. "As your attorney he needed to be warned that escrow might fall through. As your friend he wanted to know how we were going to make that happen."

She smiled into his shoulder. "Was he shocked?"

"I doubt it. I don't think there's much of anything that would shock Blayne."

"I suppose Nancy is the one to thank for that," Amanda murmured, yawning as she snuggled closer against him. "I don't have any of the details, but I've gotten the impression that their courtship was anything but normal. She was in Gstaad, I think, when they first met. She said something once that has always made me wonder if Blayne had been sent there by her father to bail her out of whatever trouble she was in."

She yawned again and closed her eyes. It was something about a lost manuscript, she thought, but couldn't put her finger on the exact circumstances. It had been eight years ago, just when she was getting Mandy's Candies up and running.

Mandy's Candies. Her eyes flickered open, and she was appalled at how close she'd come to falling asleep—now, just when she was supposed to be pacing the floor and worrying about how things were going.

It was Barley's fault, she decided, letting her eyelids

flutter shut again as she succumbed to the rhythmic stroking of his hard, warm hand. Barley's fault.

She smiled and tucked her hand under his arm.

"There's an egret out there," he said, his voice hushed in the quiet morning air. "Right next to the blue heron on that dock that has the tugboat tied up to it."

She sighed and snuggled.

"Did you know that the first time I was here, you told me to watch for egrets and I thought you were talking about monkeys?"

She mumbled something and snuggled closer.

"On Java there's a species of monkeys that are called egrets." Without changing his rhythm Biff continued to stroke her hair as he told her stories he'd never shared with another person.

Stories of fancy and fantasy that he'd made up on those long, lonely nights when he'd been roaming the world in an unknowing search for the thing he'd found with Amanda. Love. It made everything so clear, so certain.

He stroked her hair and told her stories.

She slept in his arms and dreamed of forever.

"He bit."

"You're sure?" Amanda's heart was in her throat, and she was in no condition to do something simple like invite Wyatt in. Barley did it for her, reaching past her to push the door open wide before dragging her back so that Wyatt could squeeze into the front entryway.

Wyatt smiled, a big, broad smile that made Amanda wonder why she'd ever thought that smiling wasn't something he was very good at. She allowed herself to be pushed into the living room as Barley took Wyatt's coat and hung it on the coat tree.

"I'm sure," Wyatt said, patting her on the shoulder before looking around the room and staking out the biggest, most comfortable chair for himself. It was Barley's chair, she wanted to say, but Barley pulled her down onto the sofa, and she remembered her manners.

And her curiosity. She wanted to know everything. "Tell me," she demanded. "Did he ask anything you couldn't answer? Was he suspicious? Is he going to sign?"

"No, no, and yes. We'll know for sure on Thursday."

As she'd just been awakened from a long nap in the sun—on Barley's lap—she had to take a minute to relate question to answer. Then she smiled and listened avidly as Wyatt gave them a verbatim report of the meeting.

Parks was excited, he told them. And a little arrogant, as if he'd known all along that Mandy's Candies had international potential. As it was, he'd already made plans to expand into the domestic market. But since Paradise Hotels was determined to cement the deal as soon as possible, he'd put off the local expansion in favor of the international deal.

It was, Parks had admitted, a proposition he couldn't turn down. He said he would have his lawyer look over the proposal, but he certainly didn't see anything that would stand in the way of signing the proposed agreement.

And, yes, a check drawn on Paradise Hotels would be acceptable to finalize the agreement.

After twenty minutes of Wyatt's recitation Amanda relaxed. She also realized Barley was stroking her hair as he'd done when she'd fallen asleep in his arms. She was beginning to suspect he did it on purpose.

That was okay.

"Congratulations," she said. "It sounds like you did it." She smiled at Wyatt and asked what he'd like to do until dinnertime. There was always the fossil beach, which she refused to name because only those people who'd actually been there were privileged to have that information. Or they could drive down to Hillsboro, where there was an antique show going on that week.

Or maybe he'd like a tour of Alcatraz.

Barley suggested they stay home and make Amanda rehearse her own role. She and Wyatt joined forces and dragged him out of the condominium, electing to let Barley drive. They settled in, and Wyatt asked if it were possible to see a bit of the wine country in Napa before the sun set.

It was possible. Forty minutes later they passed the first of many dozens of wineries. They stopped often, Barley playing the noble abstainer as Wyatt and Amanda sipped their way through various tasting rooms. They had a ball, the three of them acting as though they'd been friends for a decade, when it was only true of the men. It didn't seem to matter, though. Wyatt had accepted Amanda as part of Barley—or Biff, as he insisted upon calling him, to Amanda's amusement. And Biff knew that he'd never feel whole again, not if Amanda wasn't with him.

They stopped for dinner at a crowded, wonderful restaurant where they had to wait for an hour for the privilege of eating and were happy to do so. Long after dark they made the long drive back to downtown San Francisco and dropped Wyatt at his hotel. Nearly thirty minutes later Biff carried a sleeping Amanda up the stairs and into their home.

Their home. He smiled, both because she was

sleeping—again!—and because he knew she'd take issue with the phrase *their home*.

Not that she'd really mind, he knew. She'd take issue all the same because she hadn't yet let go of the idea that she was still alone.

She wasn't alone. Not by a long shot.

"Let's do something fun today."

Amanda looked at Barley over the top of the paper and asked, "So what was wrong with yesterday?"

He grinned. The day before, they'd stayed in bed—more or less. With the exception of the time they'd spent in the shower together. Not to mention the couple of minutes when he'd put on a robe to answer the door. Pizza, delivered.

And then there was the mechanic with the keys for the Husky, which he claimed was parked downstairs. Neither of them bothered to check.

Outside of those minor deviations, the day had been spent between the sheets. Or on top of them. Whatever.

"I just thought," Barley said, "you'd like to see something besides the ceiling for a change."

She snapped the paper back in front of her face so he wouldn't see the inevitable blush that colored her cheeks. "Don't be so smug, Biff. If you'd bothered to keep track, you might discover you spent as much time on your back as I did."

"Point." He grinned at the paper, then pursued his original question. "Why don't we get out of here today and play?"

"What about Wyatt?"

"You didn't ask about him yesterday."

"You didn't give me a chance," she mumbled.

"Don't worry about Wyatt. He has his own schedule until Thursday. Why don't we pack a bag and go to Tahoe for the night?"

"Just like that?" She lowered the paper and stared at him.

He grinned. "Just like that, darling. Want to give it a try?"

She looked at him suspiciously. "Give what a try?"

"Skiing, for one." He took the paper from her fingers and threw it aside. "I'll bet you'll be a regular terror on the slopes."

"What makes you say that?"

"You remind me of someone," he said, then proceeded to tell her the story of a woman he called the Turquoise Terror. She didn't believe a word of it. Nobody could be that bad at a sport and survive.

Amanda packed all the things he told her she would need, plus a couple of others he was certain she wouldn't. She threw them in anyway, because overpacking was something she did as a matter of course.

While she closed up the condo, Barley made a couple of calls. Then they piled everything into the truck and took off for the mountains.

It was only about five hours, he reminded her. They'd have plenty of time to ski that afternoon, then drive back Thursday morning so that she'd be ready for her "chance" meeting with Parks that afternoon.

She'd never skied before, she told him. Wouldn't it be better if they just watched everyone else?

It didn't matter that she'd never skied, he said. He was a terrific teacher. Besides, it was only going to be a few hours. What could possibly go wrong?

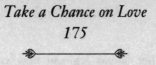

"It's not a bad break," the doctor said reassuringly. "Your own doctor will be able to put you into a walking cast as early as next week."

"Next week!" Amanda stared in dismay at the cast on the bottom half of her right leg. "But I need to walk on this tomorrow!"

"You can, Miss Lawrence," the doctor said as he backed out of the room, his gaze sliding hopefully to Barley, who was leaning against the wall with his arms crossed and his expression twisted into a scowl. When there was no help coming from that sector, the doctor shrugged and smiled weakly at Amanda. "You'll be able to get around just fine with crutches in the meantime. Your local pharmacy should have a pair for rent." He said he would send in the nurse to help her into a wheelchair and slipped out of the room.

"Crutches!" Amanda muttered something under her breath that expressed how she felt about those and glared at the cast. "How can I face Anthony on crutches?"

Barley left his place at the wall and came over to the bed where she was lying, her elbows propped up behind her so that she could see her leg. He didn't say anything, just took her hand in his and squeezed.

She shook her head dejectedly and lay back against the pillow. "This is *not* supposed to be happening to me."

He squeezed harder, but didn't interrupt her tirade. She was grateful for that. She knew enough about herself that she had to get the frustration out before she exploded.

"I had it planned down to the last detail," she said, her eyes glazing over as she remembered the vision that she would have been. Would have been, because she'd gone and broken her stupid leg and now everything had changed. "I was going to spend the morning getting a facial and having my hair done just right. And I was going to wear my cranberry silk dress—the one with the slit up the side that shows off my legs." She grimaced as she imagined just how sexy she'd look with a cast peeping out from beneath the dress.

She sighed and brought Barley's hand to her heart. It was comforting to touch him, even if it was only holding hands. "I was going to look so darned elegant that when I sashayed out of his life, he'd think twice about what he threw away." She lifted her head and looked balefully at the cast. "Sashay, ha! I'll be lucky if I don't fall on my face!" Her head bounced back against the pillow, and she shut her eyes in frustration.

It wasn't fair! Just when she'd imagined she'd be able to get a little of her own back from the man who'd dumped her, she had to go and do a stupid thing like break her leg. She rubbed Barley's hand against her cheek and wondered if he, too, was worried about the con and how convincing she'd be on crutches. He'd hardly said a word since the ski patrol had loaded her into the sled.

"I'm sorry, darling."

Her eyelids fluttered open, and she turned her head to stare at him. She noticed for the first time that his features were more harsh than usual, the lean lines of his face drawn taut with worry. "What are *you* sorry about? *I'm* the one who's mucked up everything."

Biff took a deep, shuddering breath, letting it out slowly as he studied her. She was so incredibly beautiful, even with her hair a tangled mess against the white pillow and dark circles of exhaustion beneath her eyes.

He thought about how easily she could have been

injured so much worse than she was and knew that whatever she said, he'd been wrong to bring her. She wasn't built to take the sort of risks he took for granted. He should have known better than to take a chance with her safety.

It was the last time, he told himself. From now on he'd leave the risky stuff alone when she was along. They'd watch, not do.

"It was my fault, Amanda. It wouldn't have happened if I hadn't dragged you up here in the first place."

She would have laughed if he hadn't looked so appallingly serious. "Like I'm not an adult and can't make my own decisions?"

"It was my idea. And I promised you that I was a good teacher." He eased down onto the bed beside her, careful not to jostle her leg, and lifted her hand so he could rub his lips across her knuckles. "Some teacher! I let you go and break your leg before you'd even been on skis for an hour."

"Actually I remember you saying you were a *terrific* teacher," she teased, realizing that his self-recrimination was not just a surface thing and that she'd have to do something about it before it got out of hand. "And I'm sorry to burst your bubble, but even the best teacher in the world couldn't have prevented what happened."

"You're supposed to be mad at me," he growled, his gaze narrowing on hers. "It would make me feel a hell of a lot better."

"I thought the point was for *me* to feel better." That earned her a chuckle, which went a long way toward making her feel pretty darn good. He leaned down to plant a kiss on her forehead.

"You're pretty sassy for someone who just broke her leg."

"At least we're agreed now," she said, "*I* broke my leg. You didn't do it for me."

"I still shouldn't have let you ride the lift so soon," he muttered. "I should have kept you practicing down below."

"I wanted to go up the hill," she said, shaking her head at his determination to take the blame. "You couldn't have stopped me if you'd tried."

"Still—"

She pressed her fingers to his lips. "I might not have broken my leg if I hadn't dropped my glove onto my skis. I might even have made less of a mess of it if I'd listened to you and waited until we got to the top of the hill before picking it up." She had to smile again, because the sequence of events reflected a side of her that was a long way from graceful. "But no, I had to ignore you and try to get it, even though I knew my balance wasn't good enough."

"I still could have caught you—" Her fingers pressed harder, and he stopped.

"*If* I hadn't jabbed your leg with my poles, you might have had a shot at it," she said sternly. "And I suppose *if* the T-bar hadn't whacked you on the head when I fell off the other side, there's a chance you might have been some help."

"We're just lucky the lift operators saw what was happening before someone ran over you," he said. He sucked one of her fingers into his mouth and raked it lightly with his teeth before letting it go.

"I'm still surprised how fast the ski patrol came," she said, letting her hand drop even though she would have rather kept it right where it was. The ski patrol had been upon the accident and taking care of her almost before Barley had managed to sort himself out of the tangle of equipment and limbs.

He laughed. "I think it had something to do with what you were wearing. The patrol had been hovering almost from the moment you put on your skis."

She glanced at the turquoise powder pants that were hanging over a nearby chair and frowned. She'd borrowed the outfit from Maggie, the woman behind the Turquoise Terror legend. "I don't understand. I don't look a thing like her. She's blond."

"With your hair tucked under that hat, the fact that you're a little taller than Maggie probably escaped them."

"And thus grows the legend. I suppose, though, that something good will come of my accident. As long as Maggie stays away from that outfit, she'll be able to ski with impunity. If the rumors are any good at all, everyone now thinks she's disabled."

"I'm not sure her husband will agree that's a good thing."

"At least they didn't have to cut up the pants," Amanda said, relieved because she'd wanted to make a good impression on these friends of Barley's. She didn't think that returning the ski outfit in shreds would have been a step in the right direction. The stretch pants she'd worn under the protective powder pants hadn't fared as well, however. The nurse had made mincemeat of those, completely disregarding Amanda's plea for leniency.

"What on earth am I going to wear between here and the truck?" she asked, peeking under the blanket to confirm that her legs were indeed bare—if one discounted the cast on the bottom half of one and the wool socks she'd insisted they return to her feet.

"Don't worry about it. I'll buy the blanket if I have to."

She grinned and said that would work just fine. "How's your head?"

"I'm sure a little headache has nothing on your leg." His gaze slid down to the casted limb, and he winced. "How bad is it, darling?"

"Hardly hurts at all," she said, because the pain was the last think on her mind. "Speaking of legs, what about yours? Did you have a doctor check that hole I put into it with my pole?"

He shook his head. "It's a bruise, Amanda. Nothing important." He reminded himself to be careful not to limp in front of her, though. While the bruise she'd inflicted on his thigh was more or less next to nothing, he'd pulled a muscle in his calf in an attempt not to fall on top of her when it had become clear that falling was a foregone conclusion.

"I'll be more careful the next time," she promised.

"You're sure you want to do this again?" he asked softly, his fingers threading between hers. He felt her heart thumping just a touch faster and wondered how she could consider doing something that had so far only caused her pain.

"It was kind of fun . . . up to a point." She smiled weakly. "Hard work, though. Do you think I might be a little out of shape?"

"Your shape is terrific. It's your ability to follow orders that needs work." He glanced down at her leg and shook his head. "Next time I tell you to leave something where it falls, pay attention, won't you? I don't think I could stand seeing you hurt again."

"Yes, sir. Next time I'll listen."

It occurred to them both that, thanks to her broken leg, "next time" would be months away. Next winter, most likely. Neither was willing to say what they were thinking, though, because winter was a long time into the future . . . a step toward a forever that wasn't yet assured.

The nurse came in then and gave Amanda instructions for the pain medication. They'd already given her enough to last the next few hours. Two more in four hours, the nurse said, and told her to call the hospital if the pills didn't get rid of the worst of the pain.

"If there's a problem, I'll have to call my own doctor," Amanda said, sitting up in preparation for the move to the wheelchair. "We're heading back to the Bay Area right now."

"Wrong, darling," Biff said. "We'll stay at the hotel tonight and I'll fly you back tomorrow."

She shook her head vehemently. "What if it snows and we can't get out? We *have* to be there by tomorrow afternoon. You know that."

Against his better judgment, he agreed. Her meeting with Anthony was critical, although he had his doubts that she'd be in any shape to carry it off, much less sashay anywhere.

He nodded and said, "So I'll fly us home today. Just let me call—"

"And leave the truck here? Don't be silly."

"Don't argue with me, Amanda. You're in no shape to ride that far."

Blayne would have to pinch-hit for Amanda, he'd decided. Satisfied that he'd come up with a workable solution, he was getting ready to tell her that they wouldn't go home at all, when he remembered that it wasn't his decision.

It was Amanda's business that was in jeopardy. If she was determined to get back to the Bay Area so that she could handle her part of the drama with Parks, it wasn't up to him to make it more difficult.

He was going to stand firm about the plane, though. "We can be there a lot faster if we fly."

"Listen, Biff," she said, yawning as the pain medication began to take effect. "By the time you put me into the truck, then out again and into the plane, and then out of that and into another car or whatever, one of us is going to be just a little tired. Now, if we just pop into the truck and head down the mountain, I'll probably get a lot more rest, and you won't have to lug me all over the place in the meantime."

His gaze narrowed on her face. "You don't want to fly, do you?"

She smiled and shook her head. "Nothing personal, Barley. I just think I'd rather be conscious the first time I try it."

"You've never been in an airplane?"

"Not even once."

So much for flying. He sighed and waited to see if she had anything else she wanted to argue about.

Not at the moment. Satisfied that she'd won her point, Amanda smiled at the nurse who'd been watching the byplay with undisguised interest, and said that she was ready to leave. The nurse looked disappointed, but moved to help her with the blanket and the heavy cast.

It was Barley's strong arms that she relied on, though, as she made the transition from bed to wheelchair. The nurse took over then, and he jogged on ahead with her clothes. He was pulling the truck around the curb just as she was being wheeled out. Jumping out, he pulled open the back door and noticed when he turned to her that she was fading fast.

"You'll need to sit in back, darling," he said, lifting her into his arms and taking care to support her leg. "You can stretch out that way."

"Not on your life, Biff," she said firmly, tightening her hold around his neck as the nurse wheeled the chair back into the hospital. "I get carsick, especially on winding roads." The blanket fluttered over her legs as the cold mountain air began to frost her thighs.

As he hesitated, she pressed her point. "You'll really be in a bad mood when I throw up all over your leather seats."

"Who says I'm in a bad mood now?" he growled.

"Listen to yourself," she suggested, and shivered. "You sound like a bear who just discovered his favorite berry tree was mowed down to make way for a subdivision."

"A what?" he barked.

She just smiled and lifted her brows as the satisfaction of a point proved washed over her.

"But you won't be comfortable in front," Biff argued, deliberately softening his tone even though he knew he didn't have a chance of winning the battle. She was a stubborn woman, and he was only now beginning to realize just how stubborn she could be. "The doctor said you need to keep your leg elevated."

"So get something to rest my foot on." She took his chin between her fingers and stared him squarely in the face. "I am not riding in the backseat. Understand?"

He understood. Carefully he lowered her so her one

good foot was on the ground and she was leaning against the side of the truck. He hurried around back and pulled out a couple of the smaller bags that held their clothes. After shoving these into the well of the passenger side, he pushed the seat back as far as it would go. Then he helped Amanda inside, lifting her leg to rest on the suitcases.

"That will have to do for now," he said, tucking his parka around her foot to keep it from flopping around.

"It'll do fine, Barley," she said, lying back in the reclining seat and closing her eyes. "Thanks."

He closed the door and climbed behind the wheel. She was asleep before he turned the first corner, and he wondered what difference sitting in front made.

On the way out of town he stopped at a store and bought an armful of pillows. She didn't budge as he exchanged them for the suitcases under her leg, but he thought he detected a lessening in the strain around her mouth. Either that or the pills were doing their job.

As he drove across the mountains and down into the valley on the other side, his thoughts were on the woman who slept soundly in the seat beside him.

She hadn't cried once, not when she'd broken her leg, not even when the doctor had set it. She'd held Biff's hand, though, almost squeezing tight enough to break something else.

She wouldn't let go of his hand, either, not even when the nurse had tried to shuffle him out of the room. When the nurse had insisted, Amanda had threatened to scream her head off. The doctor had clearly believed her, because he'd allowed Biff to stay.

Biff smiled and reached out to stroke her hair, lightly because he didn't want to wake her.

She'd once told him that she felt like a loser after her dealings with Parks, but she was less a loser than anyone Biff could imagine.

She won a lot more often than she gave herself credit for.

TWELVE

From his perch on the kitchen stool Biff studied the determined set of her jaw and realized that Amanda wasn't about to lose this battle either. Seated in the living room with her leg propped on the coffee table, she sipped hazelnut-flavored coffee from a dainty cup and glared across the rim at her good friend and attorney.

Blayne paced the small living room, arguing and exchanging scowls with Amanda as Wyatt sat on the sidelines and watched. Blayne was doing his best to hold his own, but the fight was going out of him. He'd been there for nearly an hour, arriving just after Wyatt, who had also been summoned by the news that Amanda wasn't exactly in top physical form for the coming drama.

Biff had arrived home with Amanda not long before midnight the previous night. She'd managed to sleep all but the last fifty or so miles and had then refused to take any more pills until she was in her own bed, saying that she needed to be awake to make the climb to her second-story condo.

She didn't want him making whatever was wrong with his leg any worse.

So much for trying to hide something from her.

He'd carried her up the steps anyway, the pulled muscle in his calf a mere tinge compared with the gigantic headache he'd been trying to ignore for the last few hours. She must have noticed that, too, because the first thing she did once they got inside was tell him where she kept the aspirin.

He'd been almost embarrassingly grateful.

The night hadn't been too bad, not for Amanda, who had immediately settled down for a long snooze after taking the pills the doctor had provided. She'd moaned in her sleep a couple of times, but it hadn't been enough to awaken her.

Between the headache that had taken hours to go away and feeling the need to keep an eye on Amanda, he'd only slept in snatches. Thus it was Biff who felt wrecked from the lack of sleep. Amanda, on the other hand, looked remarkably fresh and alert for someone who'd broken her leg less than twenty-four hours earlier.

Now, two hours before Parks was to meet with Wyatt and sign the agreement, she was holding court in her living room with every appearance of being one hundred percent in charge of the show.

Biff had to give her credit. From the way she'd been acting lately, Amanda *was* in charge. She'd only been letting him think he was running things.

He didn't mind.

Blayne gave it one last stab. "Biff and I have already discussed it, Amanda. Parks will have absolutely no reason not to believe me. In fact he'll probably be even more convinced that Wyatt is a drug lord of some sort because he won't have any reason to believe I would deliberately lie to him."

"Why should he do that? Face it, Blayne. You're a lawyer. Everyone knows lawyers are crooked."

"That's below the belt, Amanda." Biff picked up the coffeepot and carried it into the living room, where he refilled everyone's cups.

Amanda grinned sheepishly at Blayne, but sounded less than apologetic when she said, "You know I didn't mean it that way, Blayne. But look at it from Anthony's perspective. He knows you've been trying to help me get Mandy's Candies back. He has no reason to believe a word you say."

"So why is he going to believe you?"

"Because I'll use the one thing you wouldn't." She rested the coffee cup in her palm and smiled. "Hysteria, Blayne. I'll be so damned upset about what he tells me that the panic will set in before he sees it coming."

Blayne snorted, but admitted that she might have a point.

For almost the first time since he'd arrived, Wyatt spoke. "I agree with Amanda. It's her show, and if she thinks she can do it, then we shouldn't be wasting our time arguing. Her chances of convincing Parks are much better than Blayne's."

"Thanks, Wyatt." Glancing over at the big man who had once again appropriated Biff's chair, Amanda smiled. He returned it, a twitch of his lips that she'd learned to watch for because it was gone almost before it was noticed. Satisfied that she had at least one of them fully on her side, she turned back to Blayne and Barley. Barley was now sitting beside her on the sofa, while Blayne had taken another chair.

"I know it isn't going to be as elegant as I would like it, nor as simple as you'd planned it, Barley, but I see no reason why we can't carry it off with a little bit of fancy footwork."

"Fancy footwork is exactly what you can't do," he said.

She gave him a sick smile at the near-pun but otherwise acted as though he hadn't spoken. "You originally planned for me to bump into him as he came out of the bank. Or if he sent someone else to the bank, we'd do this on the street outside his office when he left for the day." They'd decided on the street because there were numerous shops in the vicinity, and he wouldn't have been suspicious about seeing her there.

She thumped her knuckles against the cast and grimaced. "Well, that's obviously not going to work now, because bumping isn't something I'm up for, not on any street."

"I guess you could just stand in his way and pretend you didn't see him coming," Barley mused. "I don't like it, though. If he's not paying attention, he'll plow into you. That's unacceptable."

Blayne and Wyatt murmured their agreement but otherwise didn't interrupt.

"On the other hand, if he does see you and you're successful in making him believe you don't see him, he might elect to avoid you altogether." He sat forward and leaned his arms on his thighs, threading his fingers together as he spoke. "We were counting on the fact that once you've actually exchanged a few fighting words, he won't be able to resist telling you about the deal with Paradise Hotels."

Blayne sat hunched over his coffee, looking as dejected as he sounded. "So all we have to do is make sure he's in a certain place at a certain time so that Amanda doesn't have to spend all day waiting. Then we have to ensure he doesn't get past her."

In one corner of the room stood the crutches that Barley had rented for her that morning. She eyed them with growing interest. A plan fell together in her mind . . . a beautiful, flawless plan. She looked at Barley to find him staring at her with a hint of suspicion in his gaze.

"What is it, darling?" he asked. "What is going on in that devious mind of yours?"

She grinned. "You know something, Barley? I think this is going to work out just fine after all."

By the time she'd told them the slight twist to the plan, even Blayne was agreeing that it had possibilities. Wyatt agreed but with modifications, then left for his meeting with Parks after calling to arrange a second, follow-up meeting that afternoon. Parks had agreed, but then, none of them had imagined he wouldn't. Wyatt was calling the tune, and Parks was dancing to it.

Blayne went back to his office because there was nothing in the current plan for him to do. He grumbled all the way out the door.

Barley brought Amanda her pills, then carried her into the bedroom so she could rest for a few hours. Showtime was four o'clock, and he didn't want her falling over her crutches because she was too tired to manage them.

Amanda suspected that falling over her crutches was something she'd probably do at one time or another, but didn't argue. As long as Barley agreed to lie down beside her, the bed was as good a place as any to pass the time. Snuggling up beside him as best she could—considering she was more or less flat on her back with her leg propped atop a couple of goosedown pillows—she sighed happily and asked him why Wyatt knew so much about the business that he was discussing with Anthony. For that matter it didn't seem like Wyatt was the type who would work for any man, much less settle for managing an import-export business.

Biff told her that Wyatt's choices were his own and to *please* go to sleep. He needed the rest even if she didn't.

They slept.

The telephone rang at one. Biff picked it up, listened for a few moments, then set it back on the receiver. Turning to Amanda, who had come wide awake at the first ring, he grinned.

"He signed."

"He did?"

"He did. This afternoon's meeting is set for three."

The second meeting had been Wyatt's idea. Presumably it was to go over a couple of the finer points of the agreement—shop design and construction, personnel and such. In truth Wyatt had suggested it because they'd had to toss out the idea of Amanda running into Parks outside of the bank or his office.

Wyatt thought it might be amusing to lay the groundwork for Amanda's claim that Paradise Hotels would be using Mandy's Candies for nefarious drug-related activities. Personnel, for example. He'd put forward his "cousin" as a manager for the Singapore shop, the first one scheduled to open. If Parks was reluctant to accommodate Wyatt's request, Wyatt was more than willing to gently twist his arm. More likely, though, Parks would be willing to do just about anything Wyatt requested.

Later, as Amanda's accusations settled in, Parks would think about that "cousin" and wonder exactly why Wyatt had been so insistent about making him manager.

The meeting would be at Wyatt's hotel, in the bar on the main floor. Amanda was to wait out of sight until she saw Barley walk past. He was the three-second warning. The next person to come around that corner would be Anthony, firmly guided into position by the ever-helpful Wyatt.

Amanda was going to use her crutches for more than walking.

Her heart suddenly beat a frantic rhythm in her chest. It was working, *really working*! But then she remembered the second half of the setup and panicked. Latching on to Barley's hand with fingers that shook, she asked, "What about the money? How can we know for sure that he'll take care of that before I see him?" She knew he'd already explained why Anthony *should* go to the bank. Suddenly, though, *should* wasn't good enough.

"Don't worry, darling." He kissed her on the nose and pried her fingers off his hand before her nails did permanent damage. "It's already in the bank. Fred followed him there right after his meeting with Wyatt."

"Who's Fred?"

"He's a private investigator I hired to keep an eye on Parks."

She stared at him blankly. "A private investigator? What on earth for?"

"Just a precaution, darling. I felt better knowing that Parks wasn't going to do something we hadn't anticipated."

The panic left her as fast as it had come, and she was amazed to find herself feeling almost relaxed. Yawning, she tucked her arms around Barley's neck as he levered her up to lean against the mound of pillows he'd arranged behind her.

Swinging his legs off the bed, he went into the bathroom and turned on the shower. When he came back into the room, he began pulling off her clothes that she'd been too lazy to remove prior to their nap.

"How it is that you're just now getting around to telling me about this Fred person?" she asked. Having had a moment to think about it, she realized that she shouldn't have been surprised that Barley would regard a private investigator as necessary to the plot. Barley wasn't the sort of man to leave things to chance.

"It wasn't worth talking about."

"You mean you didn't want to argue about it," she said, eyeing him with suspicion. "Just how much is this Fred character going to set me back?"

"He'll take care of the rest of that money you were so determined to throw away in Tahoe," Barley said, his return stare a masterpiece of innocence. "Can you think of a better way to get rid of it?"

She couldn't.

Kneeling at her feet, Barley pulled a plastic trash bag over her cast and began taping it to her leg. Then he stripped off his own clothes and helped her hobble into the shower.

She leaned against the tile wall, just out of reach of the spray. He grabbed the bar of soap and worked up a lather between his hands. "Did Wyatt ever say if Anthony called Singapore to check up on him?" she asked, her attention only half on what she was saying, because the other half was distracted by his hands as they began to stroke the soap onto her body.

He took his time. She relaxed against the cool tiles and listened as he started with her leg—the one without the cast—his fingers following the curve of her calf, massaging lightly as they traveled up and down.

"Parks called right after their first meeting. He had a scheduling problem, or so he said, and Wyatt hadn't told him where he was staying in San Francisco." Barley washed the top of her foot, then moved up her leg until her thigh was slick with suds. "The girl that we had set up to intercept the calls took care of everything."

She gasped as his fingers brushed between her legs, then frowned when he didn't repeat the caress. She felt let down. Disappointed, really, but what did she expect? They were in the shower, she had a cast on her leg, he had a bump on his head. The obstacles against doing anything more than getting clean were significantly daunting, to say the least.

Still, it was hard to think logically when he was touching her so . . . thoroughly. Yes, that was the word. Thoroughly. She took a deep breath as he cleaned the part of her other leg that was exposed above the plastic. Thoroughly.

The dull, throbbing ache in her leg almost disappeared.

"Weren't you worried," she asked, "that Anthony might have called information for the number instead of using the one off the fake business card?" It would have been so easy for it all to go wrong, she realized. One little thing like a telephone call, and she would have lost Mandy's Candies forever.

Barley murmured something that could have been

either yes or no and continued with his self-appointed task of washing her, his hands sliding over her belly and working upward. He was standing up now, and his gaze was reassuring as his hands slid around her to wash her back. "You knew there were risks that it wouldn't work when we started this. Well, darling, we've gotten past the worst of them and the con is still running. And don't worry about this afternoon because Wyatt won't take any chances at the meeting."

"I'm not worried about Wyatt," she said. "I guess I'm just worried in general. Everything is happening so fast—"

"And just last week you were impatient for things to get moving," he said, his hands closing around her breasts for just a moment before rising to smooth across her shoulders. "Now, why don't you come closer to the shower so I can wash your hair?"

Wash her hair? How could he possibly be thinking of something so practical when every nerve ending in her body was practically doing jumping jacks? She sighed in frustration and dropped her chin onto her chest in an attempt to regroup. Her gaze traveled down his body and past the ribbon of hair that arrowed downward from his belly button. When she lifted her eyes to meet his gaze again, it was with the knowledge that she wasn't the only one having difficulty remembering there was the matter of a broken leg to be considered.

His stare was hot and wanting, but with a tinge of regret that seemed to be the controlling emotion. "Not on your life, darling," he said, balancing her as he maneuvered her under the stinging spray. "There's no physical way we can do this in the shower."

"What about out of the shower?"

He chuckled and rubbed shampoo into her hair. "Ask me after your scene with Parks, darling. After all this trouble we've gone to, I'd hate to have to be the one to tell Wyatt you weren't where you were supposed to be *when* you were supposed to be there because we were making love and lost track of the time."

She hated it when he was right.

Amanda checked her watch and peeked around the corner even though Barley had told her not to. The stretch of lobby that separated her hiding place from the bar was devoid of any familiar faces—just as it should be.

There were still five excruciating minutes to go before it was to begin. She stifled a sigh of impatience and leaned against the wall. Barley had brought her a chair, but she was too nervous to sit.

She was too nervous to do much of anything but worry. She stared across the narrow hall at the bank of telephones and considered calling the bar to tell Barley she couldn't do this.

She couldn't act worth a damn. Anthony wouldn't believe her. She should have let Blayne do this part, because she'd never get through it without tripping over her lines.

She leaned on the crutches and reminded herself that stage fright was something that even the best actors had to put up with.

"Break a leg," she whispered aloud in the empty hallway, and fought the impulse to run away.

Barley had left her fifteen minutes earlier to take up his own station in the bar, the three-second warning and all that. But he'd told her not to peek, since there was always the chance that Parks would take the initiative and leave before the time scheduled for Amanda's encounter with him.

She peeked again because she couldn't resist. Nothing.

She took several deep breaths and wished she could have worn the cranberry silk dress. Broken leg and all, it was still the sexiest thing she had in her closet that was also appropriate for afternoon. She'd wanted to be at her best—sexy and pretty and downright irresistible.

The silk dress had been out of the question, though, because the crutches would have ruined it before the afternoon was over, not to mention the fact that its tight fit might have made the crutches difficult to manage.

She was, however, wearing a skirt because Barley had insisted that her cast be visible. Parks was going to have to take her word for quite a lot as it was, and Barley didn't want him to have any doubts that Amanda was in fact injured.

So she wore a skirt, a short wool one with pleats. It was emerald green, and the sweater she wore over it was a slightly lighter green with long sleeves and a V-neckline. She'd left her hair loose around her shoulders because Barley liked it that way.

It was almost time now, and the whole plan was beginning to sound ridiculous. A pay phone rang across the hall, and she watched as a woman vaulted from a nearby chair and ran to answer it. She was beginning to itch where the crutches rubbed against her sweater, the tender skin under her arms already smarting from the unaccustomed friction.

She checked her watch. It was almost time.

It took a superhuman effort not to look around the corner one last time. She was inspired, though, by the fact that Barley might be walking toward her even now, and the last thing she wanted was to get caught doing exactly what he'd told her not to do.

Remember to hang on to the back of the chair, he'd instructed. *Be sure you're balanced so that when Parks comes around the corner, you'll be able to stop him without falling over yourself.*

She studied the distance between the chair and the corner and suddenly realized that Biff had overestimated her reach. There was no way she could hang on to the chair and still get the tip of the crutch in Anthony's path. Moving the chair was complicated, thanks to the crutches and her hurry, but she managed to scoot it another foot toward the corner before she looked at her watch and realized there were only seconds to go.

She was breathing heavily as she grabbed the chair and put her full weight onto her good leg. The crutch on that side was more or less resting against the chair, too, and she levered the other one out from under her arm. They'd practiced this at home and she felt pretty stable, considering she really wasn't.

Don't hit him. Trip him. He'll know the difference.

It was such a temptation to try for both. She tightened her grip around the wooden handle and tested its weight. Grinning, she wondered what Barley would say if she speared Anthony with it—somewhere interesting. A nervous giggle parted her lips as she considered the possibilities. Was spearing by definition a sort of hitting? If so, wasn't tripping just as bad?

Apologize right up to the moment you recognize him.

She would apologize, all right. And then maybe she'd hit him again.

Remember, darling, this is for Mandy's Candies. Not revenge.

Biff didn't know everything.

THIRTEEN

Barley rounded the corner.

He hesitated for barely a second as he took in the altered setting, but she only saw reassurance in his gaze as he walked past her.

Three, two, one . . . fire.

Amanda closed her eyes and stuck the crutch around the corner. There was a sudden pressure, an oath of surprise, and she allowed the weapon to be torn from her grasp a second before she lost her balance. She heard a thud as Anthony hit the ground.

Bull's-eye.

The second thud made her eyes shoot open.

Double bull's-eye. *Oh, no!* Her thoughts gyrated with sickening speed as she realized why Barley had positioned the chair further back from the corner. Not only had she accomplished her first goal of tripping Anthony, she'd taken Wyatt down with him.

Oh, Lord, don't let him be hurt, she prayed. Barley

would never forgive her. Grunts and curses interspersed her muttered prayers. Then a man she didn't recognize arrived on the scene and calmly picked up her crutch. He handed it to her, paused long enough to make sure she was steady on her feet . . . then gave her a sly wink before disappearing back around the corner.

Fred, she presumed. She almost giggled, but stopped herself just in the nick of time because it wasn't part of the script. *Apologize right up to the moment you recognize him.* She gritted her teeth and hoped Wyatt was listening.

"Oh, no! I'm so sorry . . ." She edged toward the sprawled pair. Anthony was on the bottom, nose down on the carpet as Wyatt half lay, half sat on top of him. "It just slipped out of my hand. I'm not very good at this yet. Is anybody hurt?"

More oaths reached her ears, and she knew it wasn't only Anthony's voice that she heard. "Can you move? Shall I call a doctor? Oh, please quit swearing and say something intelligent so I'll know you're not hurt!" she demanded in a rush.

Wyatt fixed her with a look that told her he was raising his fee and started to get to his feet. He rolled off Anthony and stood, tugging his jacket back into place as he continued to stare at her. She could have sworn laughter was hiding behind his furious gaze, but with Wyatt it wasn't always easy to tell. She gulped and spread around more words of apology.

"I can't believe I did that. But these are so awkward, and I haven't had any practice." She tried to move so that she was out of the way, but Anthony chose that moment to try to lever himself up from the floor. His hand went right where her crutch was headed, and she flattened him a second time at the cost of her own balance.

"Ouch, dammit!" Anthony yelled as Wyatt scrambled across him to catch Amanda before she fell. He managed to kick Anthony in passing, and Anthony screamed again. Amanda realized they were drawing a crowd, and she hadn't even gotten started with the good part.

This was fun! she realized, but fixed a concerned frown on her face and stared down at the prone body on the floor. "Oh, my. I *certainly* didn't mean to do that. Do you think you can get up?"

"Of course I can get up," he muttered, and pushed himself to his knees. She was just considering how easy it would be to knock him backward when Wyatt gave her a warning squeeze before letting her go. He went back to stand before the kneeling Anthony and urged the crowd to disperse. "Nothing wrong here," he murmured. "A small accident, nothing more." Amanda didn't dare look at Wyatt because she was that close to laughter. Balancing on the crutches, she mouthed a few more words of apology and waited.

It wasn't long in coming.

"*Amanda!* What the hell . . . ?" Anthony scrambled to his feet and stared at her as if she'd sprouted horns. His gaze raked her top to bottom, and she gave him just enough time to take in her broken leg before she began.

"Anthony!" She backed up as though whatever was wrong with him was catching. "If I'd known it was you, I wouldn't have settled for tripping you!"

"You did this on purpose?" he sputtered.

"Of course I did," she said with a wry laugh. "I've just been waiting for you to come around the corner so I could trip you." She sneered at him. "Get real, Anthony. How was I supposed to know you'd come charging past me just then?"

He looked doubtful but let it pass. "So what happened to you?"

She glared at him and shifted her weight. "Just get out of my way, Anthony. I've already had enough go wrong this week without having to waste time talking to you."

Anthony looked only too eager to comply as he moved aside. Panicked because this was not the way it was supposed to go, she took her time organizing herself. Several seconds passed before she swung her broken leg between the crutches, then she pretended to notice Wyatt for the first time. She studied him with a puzzled expression on her face. "Don't I know you?"

Wyatt gave her the same sort of look before his expression cleared in recognition. "Amanda Lawrence! Of course, I should have put it together sooner."

Anthony's expression was rewardingly surprised.

Wyatt turned to him and said, "We met last year when . . ." His words trailed off as he shot a vaguely embarrassed glance at the still-perplexed Amanda. Shrugging, he looked back at Anthony and continued. "We met when she was still owner of Mandy's Candies. Our proposal didn't meet with quite as much enthusiasm at that point."

"You!" She let the shock wash over her, her expression almost wild in dismay. She was at a loss, not having prepared dialogue for this variation of the script. So she just said it again, putting more vehemence into it. "You!"

Wyatt took Anthony's hand and shook it. "I have another meeting, Parks. Call my secretary in Singapore if you have any questions. For now, though, I'll tell my people it's a done deal." He said good-bye and slipped away before either Amanda or Anthony could say another word.

Anthony turned back to her and shrugged. "What's your problem, Amanda? He's certainly attractive enough to warrant a bit more interest, I'd think. Or didn't you appeal to him?"

She whacked him on the side of his leg with her crutch. He yeowled loudly and bent down to pull up his pant leg.

"You've got such a filthy mind, Anthony," she spat. "Just because you suckered me into falling for you doesn't mean I chase after everything in pants."

"You're just lucky you didn't draw blood," he said, gingerly stepping on the wounded leg. "What's with you, anyway? I've never seen you so mad before."

"You're forgetting the day you stole Mandy's Candies. I remember being plenty mad then."

"But not violent," he said, his humor returning. "Breaking that leg must have altered your metabolism."

She put the lid on her boiling temper. None of this was in the script, and she couldn't risk veering too far off. "Get off my case, Anthony. Tell me instead what you're doing with scum like that."

"Scum?" He smiled. "He must have really put your nose out of joint."

She ignored the jibe and forced a panicked expression. "You're not considering his proposal, are you?"

"How do you know he proposed anything?" Still no concern.

"Wyatt Conner isn't a man to waste time with the likes of you unless there's something in it for him. Has he talked to you about expanding Mandy's Candies into Paradise Hotels? Tell me, Anthony. This is important."

Anthony looked like the cat that ate the canary.

"There's no more talking to do. As you heard him say, it's a done deal."

"You fool!" she exploded, and raised a crutch to take another whack at him. He was wise to her by this time, though, and dodged before she could follow through. *"Don't you realize what you're getting into?"*

A smidgen of concern finally appeared. "Just because you weren't able to snag a deal this big doesn't mean I would miss it."

"You *idiot!*" She stared at him and let her expression carry the full extent of her dismay. Lowering her voice to a stage whisper so that the entire lobby wouldn't hear her, she said, "Wyatt Conner and Paradise Hotels are connected at the hip with the biggest drug dealers in the Pacific! Didn't you look into this at all?"

Anthony shot a worried look over his shoulder, then practically dragged her into an adjoining conference room. Amanda sorted out her crutches and regained her balance, wishing he hadn't done that because Barley was supposed to be watching from a distance, and he couldn't see anything while they were in another room.

No matter, though. It would be over in a couple of minutes.

Anthony shut the door and turned to her. "What are you talking about? Wyatt Conner is a perfectly respectable businessman. He can sue you for saying such things."

"Respectable? Just because he wears a suit and can read?" She snorted and shook her head. "Wake up, Anthony. Conner is a crook and if you let Paradise Hotels get involved with Mandy's Candies, you're a crook too."

"How do you know?" He was really starting to look worried, but she didn't dare lessen the pressure.

"That you're a crook?" She laughed harshly. "I found out the day you stole Mand—"

"Not that," he shouted. "About Conner. How do you know he's a crook?"

Her expression was definitely exasperated. "Because I had my attorney look into the deal. Blayne didn't have to dig very deep to get the real facts on Conner. I ran as fast as I could in the other direction."

Anthony was not convinced, though. "Just for argument, why do you suppose he wants Mandy's Candies?"

"Why do you care?" she asked, her eyes wide with disbelief at such a stupid question. "Smuggling, trafficking, money laundering—any one of those would be enough to get you life plus ten in almost any state. All I know is enough to stay the hell away from it."

She let him think about it for a good minute before going on. He hadn't quite bought into it yet, but she wasn't worried. The rest of her lines were designed to make the panic override any doubts.

"At least you haven't signed anything yet," she said thoughtfully. "There's still a chance Mandy's Candies can get out of this without any real damage. No thanks to you."

"I signed," he said quietly. "This morning. I signed an agreement of intent."

"*You what?*" She blasted him with unprintable names until she ran out of them. Then she repeated the list—supplied, in part, by Barley during rehearsal—before she let an expression of hope light up her face. "I guess it might still be okay if you're willing to write off any deposit you made." She shook her head in disbelief. "Your attorney should be able to pull you out of this as long as—"

"I didn't pay a deposit. It was the other way around."

His eyes clouded with apprehension. "He gave me ten thousand dollars—incentive money, he said. I took it."

It was the bombshell of all bombshells. Amanda looked at him as though she'd never met anyone so incredibly stupid in her entire life. *"You what?"*

"I took the money." He was beginning to sweat.

"Give it back."

"He wrote me a check. It's in the bank . . ." His words trailed off as the horror of what he'd done finally hit the core.

"A paper trail." She swallowed hard, letting him see the emotion that nearly overwhelmed her. "They've got you now," she said. "You've taken drug money, and they can prove it. You'll never get away from them. Not ever."

She closed her eyes in total despair, keeping them closed a long moment before staring almost emotionlessly at him. "I should have known. Bad luck always comes in threes. First I lose management of Mandy's Candies. Then I break my leg. Now I'm going to lose Mandy's Candies altogether."

His brows furrowed in a frown. "What do you mean? You still own forty percent of Mandy's Candies."

"Not anymore," she returned. "I'll give my share away before I do business with the likes of Conner."

"I can still get out of this," Anthony said in a hurry. "Maybe I can—"

But Amanda wasn't listening. "I wonder if I can sell my shares before the news of your idiocy leaks out." She maneuvered her crutches toward the door. "If I keep the price low enough . . ."

"I'll just call Singapore and tell them—"

She ignored him. "Maybe it would be better if I just

walked away and gave up all claim on Mandy's Candies. I'll have to talk with Blayne. He'll know what to do."

"Conner's secretary will know where to find him. I'll tell him it's all been a mistake—"

Amanda shook her head regretfully. "No, it wouldn't be right selling Mandy's Candies to someone else who didn't want to deal with drugs. I wonder how I'd go about finding someone who doesn't care?"

"But I don't want to do business with drug lords," Anthony whined. "I hate drugs—"

"I suppose I could always take this opportunity to start over," she went on. "I've certainly got enough capital. And after all, once the feds get onto Mandy's Candies, I won't have any real competition."

Anthony tried to stop her from leaving the room, but she just pushed him aside with her crutch. He was babbling a mile a minute. "Conner must still be in the hotel. I'll give him cash—"

Amanda spared him a disdainful look. "Get real, sucker. Conner is going to use Mandy's Candies and then he'll bleed you dry. There's nothing you can do now except pretend to like it."

"But I'll tell him—"

"Tell him what, Anthony? That you've found out he's got drug connections that Manuel Noriega only dreamed of?" She laughed without smiling. "Does Wyatt Conner look like a man you can say those kinds of things to and walk away from?"

The gaze that met hers was filled with horror.

She rode the elevator to the eighth floor and knocked on the door of Room 812.

Barley had decided they would spend the night in town—just in case Anthony decided to pester her for more information about Wyatt Conner and Paradise Hotels. He had suggested that Barley and Wyatt take similar precautions in making themselves unavailable to Parks. Blayne was relying on his secretary to fend off all calls. Wyatt intended to leave for Singapore later that night after dinner with Barley and Amanda. In the meantime he intended to take the phone off the hook and catch a few hours' sleep. Even if Parks managed to discover where Wyatt was staying, it wouldn't do him any good.

None of the players would be reachable.

Barley opened the door and searched her face with unmasked impatience. "Well, what happened? Fred wasn't able to hear anything through that damned door."

"I think it worked," she said calmly. "I didn't blow my lines, and Anthony acted precisely as you predicted. When I left, he looked just a bit green. Hard to tell, really, in artificial light, but I know he wasn't laughing it off. In any case we won't know anything until tomorrow morning."

Barley grinned. "I knew you could do it."

"I almost botched the whole thing," she said, her face flushing as the Technicolor screen in her mind replayed the ambush in excruciating detail. "If Fred hadn't popped up when he did, I'm sure I would have said something stupid to Wyatt."

"Speaking of whom, Wyatt said to tell you you're buying dinner tonight." He stepped out of her way and urged her inside.

She winced. "I suppose that means he'll want to go to the most expensive place in town." She swung inside the room and rested on her crutches as Barley closed and locked the door behind her. It was a large, cheery room with an enormous bed at one end and a comfortable sitting area at the other. When they'd checked in earlier that afternoon, Barley had arranged things so that there was a bench in front of one of the chairs. She headed for that chair with weary determination.

"I've already booked a table in a little place down the street," he said. "It's close enough that you don't have to walk far and expensive enough to satisfy Wyatt's thirst for revenge." He followed close behind and helped her to sit before leaning her crutches in a nearby corner.

"I'm surprised he wants to see me at all."

"I think he was more embarrassed than anything. What was it he said? Something like 'When one falls into a trap that one knows has been laid, one tends to feel a bit stupid.'" Instead of going to the other chair, he sat down on the bench in front of her and settled her casted foot beside him. Reaching forward, he took her hand and cupped it between both of his.

Her breath caught in her throat as her gaze focused on his. "Do you want to hear the rest of it?" she asked, her words a whisper in the almost silent room.

His smile faded and he shook his head. "Like you said, darling, we'll know tomorrow. In the meantime I think Parks has had quite enough of your attention for one day. Let's talk about something else."

She knew that look in his eyes—the one that meant he was burning up inside and wanted nothing more than to make love with her. She knew that look because it mirrored her own feelings. Still, she saw something else in his expression—something serious that made her realize she didn't know everything that went on in his head.

"So talk, Barley. I'm listening."

"Did I ever tell you that I love how you say my name?" His fingers flexed around hers, teasing and then relaxing. "It sounds so sexy coming out of your mouth. Say it again, please."

"Barley."

He leaned forward and swallowed his name in a kiss that was so gentle, so perfect, it nearly brought tears to her eyes. A simple kiss, and she was reminded of how deeply she loved him.

Enough to let him go.

Gulping back the tears that threatened to find release, she watched as he settled back onto the bench and hoped he would make this easy, because easy or not, it had to happen.

"I love you, Barley. I want you to know that even if Anthony doesn't let go of Mandy's Candies, I appreciate all the trouble you've gone to."

"Why do I get the feeling you're about to break your promise?" he asked, his fingers threading through hers in sudden urgency.

"Promise?" It took her a minute, but then she remembered. *Forever.*

So he was going to make it hard. Her breath caught in a ragged sigh as she found his gaze with hers. "You know as well as I do that it can't work between us, Barley. You're a wanderer. I'm . . ." She tried to find a word that didn't sound so terribly stuffy, but couldn't come up with one.

"You're what, darling?"

She shrugged. "I'm not a wanderer."

He actually smiled. She found that hard to understand. "You know I'm right, Barley. We talked about it just the other night. The wanderlust. You have it and I don't."

He leaned forward, resting his elbows on his thighs and bringing her hand to his mouth. "What makes you think you don't have it, Amanda?"

A nervous laugh escaped her as she wondered if she'd heard him correctly. "Of course I don't have it, Barley. I want a stable home, a place that I can call my own."

"While I . . . ?" His voice trailed off, indicating that she should finish for him.

"While you like travel and adventure. You don't have a home and don't want one. Living like I do would drive you mad in a month." She gulped back a fresh onslaught of tears and waited for his confirmation.

His lips moved against her fingers as he spoke. "You're wrong, you know. I think a little travel and adventure sound more attractive than you're willing to admit."

Her heart started pounding in a rhythm that was definitely more upbeat than just seconds before. "A little travel, perhaps. But a lot?" She shrugged. "How can I run a business if I'm gone all the time—assuming, of course, that I'll even have a business this time tomorrow."

He refused to be diverted. "What did you plan to do when Mandy's Candies expanded? Did you think you'd be able to stay on top of the day-to-day management of all of them?"

She stared at him blankly. "I suppose I thought I'd have a manager at each, keep my on-site time to a minim—"

He broke in before she could finish. "And what were you going to do about your home? How secure are you going to feel if you don't have a home to come back to every night that you're on the road?"

Her brow furrowed as she considered that. "I'd still

have a home, a place to come back to. Not every night perhaps, but it would still be there."

"A place to come back to," he said, his expression softening as he considered it. "You know something? I think I like the sound of that."

Her heart stilled in her chest. "What are you saying, Barley?"

Biff knelt beside her chair, holding her hand over his pounding heart so that she'd know he was more afraid at that moment than he'd ever been in his entire life.

He was afraid she'd say no.

"I'm saying, darling, that I can't imagine living without you and that I'll live anywhere you ask if you'll just promise to love me forever."

"Oh, my." She stared at him, eyes wide, frantic even.

"I love you, Amanda. I want to be with you, live with you."

"Live with me?" she echoed.

"Live with you." He cleared his throat and said in a husky voice, "Marry me. Will you, Amanda? Will you marry me?"

Her mouth opened, but the only noise that came out was a faint gasp. He absorbed her surprise without commenting on it, and wished she would hurry up and say yes before his nerves shattered.

Marriage was the last thing Amanda had expected to discuss that day. *Forever*, he'd asked, but she really hadn't believed him because there was so much to keep them apart. *Forever*.

Were their differences really that important?

"But what about your work?" she finally asked, searching for a logical thing to say because everything was so incredibly emotional, and decisions couldn't be made on emotion alone.

"I can write anywhere," he said. "Naturally I'll still have to travel for research projects, but that shouldn't be for more than a couple of weeks at a time. I know that you feel secure in your home here, so this is where we'll live."

He was willing to give it up, she thought, all the exotic places he'd lived, the cultures he'd learned about from being a part of them.

She couldn't let him sacrifice the best part of what he was. She fought back. "I might not have a job—"

"So you'll get another one if you want. And if you don't, it won't matter. Grandfather was generous, even if I didn't fall in with his ambitions for me." Biff knew they could travel the world on his trust fund without either of them ever lifting a finger. Not exactly the plans he had for the money, but if that was what Amanda wanted, he'd do it.

"Not work?" She shook her head. "I can't imagine . . ."

"No, I suppose you couldn't," he agreed wryly. "You could no more be a lazy jet-setter than I could."

"I work long hours."

"So do I," he returned without missing a beat. He held her gaze with his, refusing to let her look away because he knew that the only chance they had was here and now.

Tomorrow, when she had Mandy's Candies back and was once again immersed in its management, she might find it easier to say no. Tomorrow, when she'd had time to think about it, she might doubt that he could be happy living in one place.

Hell! Tomorrow he might have his own doubts. But

he knew one thing for certain, and that was the driving force behind the issue he was insisting upon. He would love Amanda forever and would need her through eternity.

That love and need would always be stronger than anything else that might influence his life.

He was determined to make her understand that.

It was everything she wanted, Amanda thought, so why was she trying to talk him out of it? Barley, living with her. Loving her. *Staying with her.*

She'd never have to say good-bye, not for any longer than it took him to travel somewhere far away, do his research, and come back. In return she had to give nothing . . . except love.

It was all he asked.

"Forever?" she asked, just in case she hadn't understood.

"Forever, darling. Just say the word."

She nodded. "In that case I have a counterproposal."

He lifted a single brow as if only marginally interested.

"First, you have to get off your knees."

"You haven't said yes yet."

"Then, yes, darling," she said, the tears finally brimming. "Now get off your knees before you freeze in that position."

Biff hid the wince that was the result of kneeling, not because his manly pride was at stake but because he knew she'd tease him about it in the years to come. Creaking knees was not how he wanted her to remember his proposal. Shifting her cast to the far side of the bench, he sat down and reclaimed her hand in his.

Her ringless hand. They'd go shopping that evening,

after they made love, before dinner. Union Square was filled with jewelers. They'd shop until they found what she wanted.

Or maybe he'd make love to her and sneak out while she was sleeping.

"What if . . ." She paused, took a deep breath, and started again. "Assuming I get Mandy's Candies back, what if I go with you when you do research? Like you said, I was planning on hiring a manager anyway . . ."

"You'd go with me?"

"If you want me to. In fact I see no reason we can't go for more than a couple of weeks."

He grinned. "Darling, I think you're getting carried away. What happens to the children if we disappear for months at a time?"

"Children?"

He nodded. "It's going to put a crimp in our travel plans, but I think that's the natural order of things."

"Children," she said, accepting the idea with the barely restrained enthusiasm of a person who knew exactly what she wanted. Her smile flashed, and she leaned forward for a kiss. "What is it about the word *children* that makes me feel like I want to find out if this cast is going to come between us or not?"

He grinned, and showed her that a mere cast was no hindrance at all.

It wasn't until they were rushing out to meet Wyatt that Biff remembered the ring.

Tomorrow, he told himself. And he smiled because tomorrow was a day he'd enjoy for the rest of his life . . . for the rest of their lives together.

FOURTEEN

Wyatt took their news with another of his enigmatic looks—the smile that wasn't quite there and a few congratulatory words that were designed to let them know he'd been expecting this all along and wasn't the least bit surprised.

He was, however, gracious enough to order Taittinger and pay for it.

"I had a call just before I left the room," he said after the third toast.

"I thought you weren't supposed to answer the phone," Biff growled.

Wyatt held up his hand in a motion that begged silence. "It was Blayne. I'd ask him to check in before we went out for dinner." He helped himself to a piece of toast covered with a pâté of unrecognizable ingredients that Barley had insisted would go well with champagne.

"And?" Amanda considered throwing her glass at him and would have . . . but, after all, it was Taittinger, and one didn't waste it.

"And he's heard from Parks."

"*He* answered the phone!" Biff exploded. No one was being unavailable like they were supposed to. "How can we expect to pull this off if everyone—"

Wyatt did that thing with his hand again, and Biff softened his griping to a dull murmur.

"So what did Blayne say?" Amanda asked, not the least put off by Wyatt's obvious control and Barley's lack of it.

"He said, dear Amanda, that he's in receipt of a letter from Parks in which he declines to complete the purchase of Mandy's Candies. The earnest money of course is nonrefundable—"

His voice was lost beneath the whoops of excitement around him. Amanda hugged Wyatt first—the bearer of good tidings—then Barley, then hugged them both again for good measure.

Biff saluted Wyatt with his glass and ordered another bottle. Wyatt almost cracked a smile, but when he noticed the tears on Amanda's face, he seemed to retreat from showing any emotion other than concern. Biff saw the look Wyatt gave Amanda, and for the first time, noticed her tears.

"Not to worry," he assured his friend. "I have it on the best authority that she cries when she's happy."

Wyatt was unconvinced, but decided that Biff—or was it Barley?—knew what he was talking about.

After dinner, when they were lingering over coffee, Amanda got her first inkling that Anthony wasn't the only one who'd been conned.

"So, Amanda," Wyatt said. "Now that you have Mandy's Candies back, what are your plans?"

Six weeks since she'd last walked into the shop, and the Lord only knew what damage had occurred in the meantime. She decided to think positively, though, because she had it back, and nothing else mattered. "I guess I'll go on like before," she said. "Maybe in a few years I'll get enough ahead to try expanding on my own. In the meantime . . ." She looked at Barley and smiled. "In the meantime there's lots more to keep me busy than making petits fours."

Wyatt coughed into the intimate exchange and checked his watch. He was running out of time and decided to rush in where Barley would perhaps have had him break it to her a little easier.

"Amanda, have you ever considered taking Mandy's Candies international?"

"Yeah, sure!" She giggled and sipped her coffee. "You might be able to make Anthony buy that line, but I've seen it from the other side, and I'm not interested."

Barley squirmed in his chair and refused to look at her. As a result she pinned Wyatt with her suspicious gaze. "What's up, Wyatt? You've succeeded in making Biff wish he'd excused himself to the men's room, and I want to know why."

Biff knew he was in trouble. She hadn't called him Biff in days.

"It was my idea, Amanda," Wyatt began. "When Biff called me about the con—"

"What do you mean, your idea? I could have sworn it was Biff's."

"Biff had the idea," Wyatt agreed, "but when he

asked me to participate, I suggested you'd find it easier if you thought we were all playing a game. Not just you."

"What do you mean?" Her gaze narrowed, and she almost laughed at the sudden image of Wyatt as a money-slinging drug lord.

It was ludicrous, and she told him so. A casting coup nevertheless, considering how much he looked the part.

"Not that, Amanda," he said, but thanked her for not jumping to that particular conclusion. "It's the other thing. I'm really not an import-export manager."

She gave him a forgiving smile. "Of course you're not. I never really believed that part." She didn't know what he was, but it was nice that he was fessing up.

She didn't care if he was a used-car salesman or a retired astronaut. Wyatt was whatever he wanted to be, and that was that. "Do tell me, though. I've been dying of curiosity."

Biff groaned and summoned their waiter for more coffee.

"I'm really the CEO of Paradise Hotels."

She blinked. "CEO?"

"CEO is just a title he uses when he's in public," Biff said, shooting murderous looks at the man he'd thought was his friend. Amanda was going to kill him for this.

He looked up to find he now had her attention but not Wyatt's. "Chief executive officer is how most everyone knows him. There are a very few who also know he's sole owner of all Paradise Hotel properties."

She stared at Biff. "And you didn't think I needed to know?"

"Like he said, it was his idea."

The expression she shot Wyatt was definitely censuring. "You thought it would be easier if I thought we were all playing a game?"

Wyatt shrugged. "All of which doesn't get us to the point that I wanted to talk—"

"You didn't steal any stationery?" she asked.

"Didn't have to."

"The secretary who answered the phone . . ."

"Was mine."

"The check for ten thousand dollars . . ." She shuddered and took a gulp of her coffee.

"There was an order to stop it should Parks not cancel escrow proceedings with Mandy's Candies," Wyatt said, patting her on the hand. "But none of this is what I want—"

Amanda tried the same hand gesture he'd used on Biff earlier with such effective results. It worked. "Why on God's earth did you think I'd let you get involved with something like this? You're a respected man, Wyatt Conner, with a sizable business." She shook her head in disbelief. "It's bad enough that Biff had to think up this charade. But you . . . you have much better things to do than masquerade as an international drug dealer, trafficker . . . whatever! What are you doing wasting your time—"

It was his turn to use "the hand." "I wasn't wasting time for even a second, Amanda. Now, hush because I have to leave for the airport in about five minutes and I need to ask you something."

"What?" Barley and Amanda chorused.

"It's about Mandy's Candies." He waited until he was certain he had their total attention. "What if I told you there was an opening for a shop just like yours . . . ?"

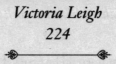

"I had no idea he'd do that."

"Barley, shut the door." She'd quit calling him Biff just a few minutes earlier . . . about the same time he'd suggested that having a Mandy's Candies in Singapore would certainly expand their horizons. More than a couple weeks' of travel, he'd pointed out.

"Honestly, Amanda. I didn't put him up to it."

"Of course not, darling," she said, throwing her crutches in his direction and flopping back onto the bed without worrying if he was going to catch them or not. "You're not devious enough to plan something like that."

He stacked the crutches in the corner and came toward her, tugging his shirt out of his pants as he walked. "I'm beginning to think you've been in charge of this con from the very beginning."

She giggled and told him to hurry up and get undressed. He complied.

"There was something about that woman in Tahoe," he said, bending over to pull off her shoe. "It was as though she looked across the room and knew me."

"A sucker isn't hard to spot."

"I never said you were a sucker," he grumbled. "Beautiful, yes. But a sucker, never."

"I was talking about you," she said, then screamed with laughter as he tickled the underside of her foot. "But I guess you'd know all about snap judgments, Barley. You were convinced there was something happening to us from the very beginning . . . whereas I never knew what hit me!"

He fell down beside her on the bed and cradled her in his arms. "It's nice to know I got something right."

She shifted onto her hip. Smiling that secret kind of smile that only lovers share, she said, "I'm so grateful you believed in that something . . . enough to work at it."

He rolled onto his back and took her with him, cushioning her broken leg between his thighs. "Work, Amanda?" He laughed and raised his head to kiss her. "No, darling. This isn't work. This is what I call pleasure." He cupped her head with his hand and urged her lips down to his. "And you felt it too. You've already confessed that much, Amanda. Don't start lying to me now."

"Lie to you, Biff, darling?" She took his lower lip between her teeth and inflicted only semipermanent damage. He was gasping for . . . well, something, when she finally let go. "I'd never lie to you, Biff. Not like you and Wyatt—"

"Not my fault! Wyatt really wanted—"

"What Wyatt wants isn't what I'm concerned with right now," she said, and shimmied against the totally male body beneath her, her broken leg not even a thought as she concentrated on Barley. "Love me, darling," she whispered. "Love me forever."

"I promise." His hands sought the gap between her sweater and skirt, and he made a start on his promise of forever.

His heart, her heart were already entwined in a never-ending dance of love. The pleasures of the body were mere extensions of that dance.

She strained against him and wondered at the natural symmetry of man and woman.

Her man.

His woman.

Mandy's Candies.

Forever.

THE EDITOR'S CORNER

Dear Readers,

If you loved our **BAD BOYS** last year, wait till you get a taste of our November LOVESWEPTs: **DANGEROUS MEN**! From a mysterious undercover state trooper to a roguish football player and a wilder-than-wild oil field wildcatter, these men thrive on danger, live on the edge, and push passion right past the limit! Like our heroines, you'll find it impossible to resist the sheer thrill of a walk on the wild side with men who are definitely *not* what your mother had in mind! With bold seduction and promises of passion, November's six heroes will sweep our heroines—and you—off your feet and into the fantasy of being loved by a Dangerous Man. . . .

Leanne Banks has created our first Dangerous Man in the sultry tale she calls **DANCE WITH THE DEVIL, LOVESWEPT #648**. Garth Pendleton was a bad boy who was definitely out of Erin Lindsey's league. Everything about him was a dare and Erin trembled at the danger of caring for a man whose darkest secret was tangled with her own shadowed past. Garth felt he'd waited for Erin forever and wanted to give her back her lost dreams, but if she knew the pain that haunted him, he feared the woman who'd slipped inside his lonely heart might slip away. This tempting tale is sure to please all of you who helped to make Leanne's January 1993 LOVESWEPT a #1 bestseller.

Doris Parmett's electrifying heroes and heroines have never been so highly-charged as they are in **BAD ATTITUDE**, LOVESWEPT #649. Reid Cameron was a heartbreaker cop who kissed like the hero of a hot romance. He'd invaded Polly Sweet's privacy—and her fantasies—when he'd commandeered her house to catch a jewel thief, but when he decided they'd play lovers and then tried to teach the feisty spitfire a lesson about feigning passion, both were shocked by the fireworks their lips set off! Doris is in top form with this sizzling story.

Longtime favorite author Patt Bucheister will tempt and tease you to distraction with her **TAME A WILDCAT**, LOVESWEPT #650. Ryder Knight had always thrived on the adventure of being a wildcatter, relished the pursuit of a new oil well, but he felt his restlessness vanish when Hannah Corbett told him he looked like trouble—and that he was no gentleman! But when his possessive embrace made her go up in flames, she feared losing control, trading her freedom for the joy only he could teach her. Patt will keep you on the edge of your seat for every page of this one!

We at LOVESWEPT are always pleased to welcome a talented new writer to our pages, and we're sure you'll agree that Donna Kauffman, author of

ILLEGAL MOTION, LOVESWEPT #651, is as good as they come. Football star Nick Logan was desperate enough to try anything to clear his name, and he figured he could intimidate or charm the truth out of Willa Trask—until he was burned by the sparks that flared between him and the beautiful redhead! He'd hired her to rehabilitate his injured knee, vowing to discover if she'd helped frame him—but instead of an ice princess, he found in her a wanton witch who touched his soul. When you've read this winning story, I'm sure you'll become big fans of Donna Kauffman!

We turn from a rookie to an all-star pro for our next Dangerous Man. Let the heartbreaking emotion of Laura Taylor sweep you away with **WILDER'S WOMAN**, LOVESWEPT #652. Craig Wilder—uncivilized, untamed, he'd paid a high price for survival. He'd meant to teach Chelsea Lockridge a lesson, to punish his ex-wife for her betrayal, but he hadn't anticipated the erotic torment of molding his body to hers—nor imagined the tenderness still buried deep inside his battered heart! She'd braved the wilderness and a storm with evidence that could deliver the justice Craig had been denied, but Chelsea wanted to prove she'd never lost faith in him . . . or her reckless passion for the man who could make her purr with pleasure. Branded for all eternity by a lover whose scars ran deep, she vowed she could help Craig mourn the past and trust her again by fighting his demons with the sweet fury of her love. Laura's deeply moving tale will capture you, heart and soul.

If you like your men *truly* dangerous, Glenna McReynolds has the mystery man for you in **AVENGING ANGEL**, LOVESWEPT #653. Bruised and bloody, Dylan Jones has driven a thousand miles with her name on his lips, desperate to save Johanna Lane from being murdered! The secrets she knew made her a target, and he was her best chance of getting out alive—even if it meant abducting the lady and keeping her with him against her will. Frightened and furious, Johanna was stunned to realize she knew her captor . . . and once had even desired him! Dylan gambled his life to feel her heat and taste the forbidden fruit of her lips and Johanna longed to repay the debt. I can't think of a better way to end your month of **DANGEROUS MEN** than with Glenna's **AVENGING ANGEL**!

So hang on to your hearts—next month six **DANGEROUS MEN** are coming to steal them away!

Happy reading,

Nita Taublib

Nita Taublib

Associate Publisher

P.S. Don't miss the exciting women's fiction Bantam has coming in November—sensual seduction in Susan Johnson's **OUTLAW**; love and black magic over the centuries in **MOONLIGHT, MADNESS, AND MAGIC** by LOVESWEPT authors Suzanne Forster, Charlotte Hughes, and Olivia Rupprecht; and a classic Fayrene Preston romance, **SATIN AND STEELE**. We'll be giving you a sneak peek at these terrific books in next month's LOVESWEPTs. And immediately following this page, look for a preview of the spectacular women's fiction books from Bantam *available now!*

Don't miss these exciting books by your
favorite Bantam authors

On sale in September:
A WHISPER OF ROSES
by Teresa Medeiros

TENDER BETRAYAL
by Rosanne Bittner

THE PAINTED LADY
by Lucia Grahame

OREGON BROWN
by Sara Orwig

And in hardcover from Doubleday
SEIZED BY LOVE
by Susan Johnson

Teresa Medeiros

nationally bestselling author of
ONCE AN ANGEL
and HEATHER AND VELVET

presents

A WHISPER OF ROSES

"From humor to adventure, poignancy to passion,
tenderness to sensuality, Teresa Medeiros writes rare
love stories to cherish."—*Romantic Times*

*Set in the wild Highlands of Scotland, this captivating
historical romance is bursting with the breathtaking passion,
sparkling humor, and enchanting atmosphere that have
made Teresa Medeiros a bestselling author. It tells the
heartbreaking tale of two lovers torn between their passion
and the clan rivalry that divides their families.*

The door behind him crashed open into the opposite wall,
and Morgan swung around to find himself facing yet
another exotic creature of myth.

A princess, her cloud of dark hair tumbled loose around
her shoulders, the light behind her throwing every curve
beneath her ivory nightdress into magnificent relief. Her
delicate fingers were curled not around a scepter, but
around the engraved hilt of a ceremonial claymore.

Silvery fingers of moonlight caressed the five feet of
steel that lay between her hands and his heart.

"Hold your ground, rogue MacDonnell," she sweetly
snarled. "One careless step and I'll be forced to take your
head downstairs without the rest of you."

Morgan didn't even feel the pain as the crystal rose

snapped in his clumsy hands, embedding its stem deep in his palm.

"Why, you clumsy oaf! Look what you've gone and done now!"

Morgan's gaze automatically dropped to his hands. A jagged shard of glass protruded from his palm. Warm blood trickled down his wrist and forearm to puddle on one of Elizabeth Cameron's precious rugs. Before he could quench it, the old shame flared. Shame for being a MacDonnell. Shame for being such a crude ox. Just as quickly on its heels followed rage—the crushing rage that shielded his tattered pride from every blow. But before he could unleash it on the hapless girl, she dropped the sword and rushed over to him.

Tossing the splintered remains of the rose aside without a second glance, she cradled his hand in hers and dabbed at the wound with a wad of her nightdress. Her little hand was warm and soft and silky smooth beneath his own. "You really should take more care," she chided. "If you'd have struck your wrist, you might have bled to death."

Morgan was too dumbfounded by her concern to point out her illogic. If she'd have cut off his head, he might have bled to death even quicker. Still scowling over his hand, she dragged him toward the pale circle of light at the window.

"Be very still," she commanded. "I'm going to try to fish out this piece of glass. It's bound to be painful. You may scream if you like. I shan't think any less of you."

Since she'd never thought much of him to begin with, Morgan wasn't concerned. He didn't even flinch when she pressed his palm with her thumb and snagged the sliver of glass between the polished crescents of her fingernails.

Thoroughly bemused, Morgan studied her in the moonlight. The top of her head barely came to his chest. The spiral curls he used to yank with such relish tumbled down her back in inky waves. Her skin was fair except for the faintest hint of color, as if God had brushed rose petals across her cheeks and lips. A fringe of ebony silk shuttered her eyes. Her scent filled his nostrils, and he was shocked to feel his throat tighten with a primal hunger. She smelled like her mother, but fresher, sweeter. Some primitive male instinct warned him this was a bloom still on the vine, fragrant and tender and ripe. He frowned. She might be nectar to another man, but to him, Dougal Cameron's daughter would be as deadly as nightshade.

Her teeth cut into her lower lip as if to bite back a cry of her own as she drew forth the shard of glass and stanched the bleeding with yet another wad of her nightdress. Morgan feared he might soon have more of it twined around his arm than she had around her body. But an intriguing glimpse of a slender calf silenced his protest.

Grimacing, she lay the bloody splinter on the window-sill before glancing up at him.

At that moment, he cocked his head to the side, giving her an unobstructed view of his face. Moonlight melted over its harsh planes and angles, etching its alien virility in ruthless lines. He was a stranger, yet so hauntingly famil-iar she couldn't stop her hand from lifting, her fingertips from brushing the stubborn jut of his jaw. His eyes were guarded, like the forest at dusk.

"Hello, brat," he said.

Then she felt that old, familiar kick in the stomach and knew she was standing face to face in the moonlit tower with Morgan MacDonnell, his boyish promise of mascu-line beauty come to devastating fruition.

Mortified by her own boldness, she snatched her hand back, remembering another time she had touched him in tenderness and he had rubuked her in anger.

A wry grin touched his lips. "I suppose if you'd have known it was me, you'd have let me bleed to death."

Terrified she was going to revert to a stammering six-year-old, she snapped, "Of course not. You were dripping all over Mama's Flemish rug."

To hide her consternation, she lowered her gaze back to his hand. That was a mistake for she could not help staring, fascinated by the blunt size of his fingers, the warmth of his work-roughened skin, the rhythmic throb of his pulse beneath her thumb. She had the absurd thought that it must take a mighty heart indeed to fuel such a man.

"You've grown," she blurted out accusingly.

"So have you."

His low, amused tone warned her. She looked up to find his gaze taking a leisurely jaunt up her body, finally coming to rest with bold regard on her face. A splinter of anger twisted in her heart. For so long she had yearned for him to look at her with affection. But why now, when she sensed his admiration might be even more lethal to her than enmity?

Hardly aware of her actions, she tore a strip of priceless Chinese silk from her mother's drapes and wrapped it around his palm. "So what were you doing up here? Plotting a massacre? Trying to find a way to lower the harpsichord out the window? Searching for a mouse to put in my bed?"

Lucky mouse, Morgan thought, but he wisely refrained from saying so. "If you must know, lass, I was searchin' for a moment's peace."

"Ha!" She knotted the bandage with a crisp jerk that finally drew a flinch from him. "Peace and the MacDonnells hardly go hand in hand."

"Fine talk from a lass who just burst in here threatenin' to cut off my head."

Sabrina could hardly argue with the truth of that.

He jerked his head toward the door. "Why aren't you down there with the rest of your family, lordin' your noble gestures over the poor peasants?"

Morgan's size might have changed, but not the rest of him. Resenting his uncanny knack of making her feel ashamed of who she was, she gave a dainty snort. "Peasants, indeed. Barefoot savages, the lot of them. Mama would have been better off serving them at a trough instead of a table."

His voice was quiet, its very lack of emotion a rebuke of its own. "If their table manners aren't to your likin', it might be because most of them won't see that much food again in their lifetimes. And their feet are bare because they're savin' the rotted soles of their boots for the cold winter months. They don't lose as many toes that way."

Shame buffeted her. Sabrina dropped her gaze, then wished she hadn't as it fell on the stark lines of Morgan's bare legs and feet. Golden hair dusted his muscular calves. His soles must be as tough as leather to bear the stony soil of the mountainside without protection. Her own toes curled sheepishly into the plush cashmere of her stockings.

"I begged Mama to let me join the festivities," she confessed.

"Why didn't you appeal to your dotin' papa? As I recall,

he never could resist a flutter of those pretty little lashes of yours."

Sabrina's gaze shot to his face. Morgan had never given her any indication that he'd noticed her lashes before. "Even Papa was adamant this time." A soft chuckle escaped her. "It seems your reputations preceded you. He was terrified one of you might hit me over the head and drag me off by my hair."

Morgan was silent for so long that she feared she'd offended him again. Then he reached down and lifted a skein of her hair in his uninjured hand, rubbing it between thumb and forefinger. A dreamy languor stole across her features. The cadence of Sabrina's heartbeat shifted in warning.

He let the stolen tendril ripple through his fingers in a cascade of midnight silk before turning the dusky heat of his gaze on her. "I can't say I blame him, lass. If you were mine, I'd probably lock you away, too."

If you were mine . . .

The words hung suspended between them, far more awkward than their silence. In a breath of utter lunacy, Sabrina wondered how it would feel to belong to a man like him, dared to ponder what came after being dragged off by her hair.

Caught in the same spell of moonlight and solitude, Morgan's gaze dropped to her parted lips. His starving senses reeled, intoxicated by the scent of roses that flared his nostrils, the cling of her hair against his callused knuckles. He'd long ago resigned himself to the harsh life of a Highland warrior. But this girl's softness awakened old hungers and weakened his resolve. He hadn't touched a drop of wine, yet he felt drunk, reckless. What harm could one kiss to? Resisting the temptation to plunge his tongue between her unwitting lips, he leaned down and touched his mouth to hers.

At the press of Morgan's lips against her own, Sabrina's eyes fluttered shut. His kiss was brief, dry, almost tentative, yet a melting sweetness unfolded within her. She felt the leashed power in his touch. Such gentleness in a man his size wove a spell all its own. Only in the last brief second of contact did he allow himself the wicked luxury of dragging his lips across hers, molding her beneath him in perfect harmony.

TENDER BETRAYAL
by
ROSANNE BITTNER

Bestselling author of OUTLAW HEARTS
and THUNDER ON THE PLAINS

"Bittner's characters are so finely drawn, their lives so richly detailed, one cannot help but to care deeply for each of them." —*Affaire de Coeur*

When Audra Brennan savored her first, forbidden taste of desire in the arms of handsome lawyer Lee Jeffreys, his caresses sparked a flame within that burned away the differences between rebel and Yankee.

The shelling from the bigger guns seemed to have stopped. She decided that at least until daylight she had no choice but to stay here as Lee had directed. She went back to the cot and lay down, breathing his scent on his pillow and sheets. How odd that she felt so safe in this bed where a Yankee soldier slept. She was in the center of the enemy camp, yet she was not afraid.

She drifted off to sleep, losing all track of time. Finally someone knocked gently on the rear door. "Audra? It's me."

Audra rubbed at her eyes, holding the shirt around herself as she found her way to the door. It was still dark. "Lee?"

"Let me in. The worst is over."

Audra obeyed, and Lee turned and latched the door again. Audra looked up at him, seeing blood on his right arm. "You're hurt!"

"Nothing drastic. I told my commander I'd tend to it

myself. He doesn't know you're in here, and I don't want him to know just yet." He threw a bundle of clothes on the small table on which the lamp was sitting. "I looted those out of a clothing store like a common thief. I don't know your size. I just took a guess. You've got to have something to wear when you leave here."

Lee removed his jacket and boots, then began unbuttoning his shirt. "It's a madhouse out there. Most of the men have chased the rebels back into the countryside, and they're looting through town like crazy men. It's practically impossible to keep any of these men in line. They aren't regular army, just civilian volunteers, for the most part, come here to teach the rebels a lesson. They don't know a damn thing about real military conduct or how to obey orders." He glanced at her. "I still intend to have the bastards who attacked you whipped. How do you feel?"

She sat down on the cot, suddenly self-conscious now that she was more rested. She had removed her shoes and stockings and wore only his shirt and her bloomers. "Just terribly tired and . . . I don't know . . . numb, I guess. It's all so ugly and unreal."

"That's war, Audra, ugly and unreal. You asked me once what it's like. Now you know." He peeled off his bloodstained shirt, and Audra found herself studying his muscular arms and the familiar broad chest, the dark hair that lightly dusted that chest and led downward in a V shape past the belt of his pants. He walked to the stand that still held a bowl of water and he poured some fresh water into it, then wet a rag and held it to the cut on his arm, which was already scabbing over. "Some rebel tried to stab me with his bayonet. Missed what he was aiming for by a long shot, but he didn't miss me all together, obviously."

"Let me help you."

"Don't worry about it. It isn't bleeding anymore." He washed his face and neck, then dried off and picked up a flask of whiskey. He opened it and poured some over the cut, grimacing at the sting of it. Then he swallowed some of the whiskey straight from the flask. "They say whiskey is supposed to help ease pain," he said then. "It does, but only physical pain. It doesn't do a thing for the pain in a man's heart."

She looked away. "Lee, don't—"

"Why not? In a couple of days you'll go back to Brennan Manor, and I'll go on with what I have to do, because I'm bound to do it and it isn't in me to be a deserter, no matter the reason. You have to stay near home because it's the only way you're going to know what happened to Joey, and you'll want to be there when he comes home, God willing. Who knows what will happen when all this is over? In the meantime I've found you again, and I need to tell you I love you, Audra. I never stopped loving you and I probably never will."

Audra held back tears. Why was he saying this now, when it was impossible for them to be together? Everything had changed. They were not the same people as they'd been that summer at Maple Shadows, and besides that, it was wrong to be sitting here half-undressed in front of the man she'd slept with while married to someone else, wasn't it? It was wrong to care this much about a Yankee. *All* of this was wrong, but then, what was right anymore?

He set the flask down on the table. "This might really be it, Audra; the end for you and me. But we have tonight."

"Why is it always that way for us? It was like that at Maple Shadows, and that one night you came to visit. All we ever have is one night, Lee, never knowing what will come tomorrow. I can't do that again. It hurts too much, and it's wrong."

Audra looked away as Lee began to undress. "Please take me somewhere, Lee, anywhere away from here."

He came over to kneel in front of her, grasping her wrists. "There *is* no place to take you, not tonight. And it's *not* wrong, Audra. It was *never* wrong, and you know it. And this time it isn't just tonight. When this is over, I'm coming back, and we're going to be together, do you hear me? I'm not going to live like this the rest of my life. I want you, Audra, and dammit, you want *me*! We've both known it since that first day you came here to see me, widow or not! Maybe this *is* the last chance we'll have to be together, but as God is my witness, if I don't get killed or so badly wounded that I can't come to you, I'll be back to find you, and we're going to put this war behind us!"

She looked at him pleadingly. "That's impossible now," she said in a near whisper.

"That isn't true. You just don't want to *believe* that it's possible, because it makes you feel like a traitor." He leaned closer. "Well, then, *I'm* a traitor, too! Because while my men are out there chasing and killing rebels, I'll be in here making *love* to one!"

Why couldn't she object, argue, remember why she should say no? Why was she never able to resist this man she should have hated?

"I never said anything about making love," she whispered.

He searched her green eyes, eyes that had told him all along how much she wanted him again. "You didn't have to," he answered.

THE PAINTED LADY
by
LUCIA GRAHAME

This is a stunningly sensual first novel about sexual awakening set in nineteenth-century France and England. Romantic Times *called it "a unique and rare reading experience."*

This wonderfully entertaining novel showcases the superb writing talents of Lucia Grahame. With lyric simplicity and beauty THE PAINTED LADY will entrance you from first page to last. Read on to discover an exquisite story about a proud, dark-haired woman and her hidden desire that is finally freed.

"If I stay longer with you tonight," Anthony said, his words seeming to reach me through a thick mist, "it will be on one condition. You will not balk at *anything* I ask of you. I leave it to you. I will go now and count tonight to your account, since, although you were occasionally dilatory, you acquitted yourself well enough, for the most part. Or I will stay, on *my* conditions—but at *your* wish. It rests with you. Do I stay or go?"

"Stay," I whispered.

I swayed and jingled as he led me back to the hearthside and laid me down upon the pillows.

"Undress me," he commanded when we were stretched out before the fire. "Slowly. As slowly as you can."

I moved closer to him and began to unfasten the buttons of his waistcoat.

He sighed.

"Don't rush," he whispered. "I can feel how eager you are, but try to control yourself. Take your time."

It was maddening to force myself to that unhurried

pace, but in the end it only sharpened my hunger. As I contemplated the climactic pleasures in store—who could have said how long it would take to achieve them?—I could not help savoring the small but no less sweet ones immediately at hand. The slight drag against my skin of the fine wool that clothed him, more teasing even than I had imagined it; the almost imperceptible fragrance of lavender that wafted from his shirt, the hands which lay so lightly upon my waist as I absorbed the knowledge that the task he had set for me was not an obstacle to fulfillment but a means of enhancing it.

Yet I had unbuttoned only his waistcoat and his shirt when he told me to stop. He drew back from me a little. The very aura of controlled desire he radiated made me long to submerge myself in the impersonal heat and forgetfulness that his still presence next to me both promised and withheld.

I moved perhaps a centimeter closer to him.

"No," he said.

He began, in his calm, unhasty way, to remove his remaining clothing himself. I steadied my breath a little and watched the firelight move like a sculptor's fingers over his cool, hard body.

At last he leaned over me, but without touching me.

"You're so compliant tonight," he said almost tenderly. "You must be very hungry for your freedom, *mon fleur du miel*."

I felt a twist of sadness. For an instant, I thought he had used Frederick's nickname for me. But he had called me something quite different—a flower, not of evil, but of sweetness . . . honey.

He brought his hand to my cheek and stroked it softly. I closed my eyes. Only the sudden sharp intake of my breath could have told him of the effect of that light touch.

He bent his head. I caught the scents of mint and smoke and my own secrets as his mouth moved close to mine.

I tipped my head back and opened my lips.

How long I had resisted those kisses! Now I craved his mouth, wanting to savor and prolong every sensation that could melt away my frozen, imprisoning armor of misery and isolation.

He barely grazed my lips with his.

Then he pulled himself to his knees and gently coaxed me into the same position, facing him.

Keeping his lips lightly on mine, he reached out and took my shoulders gently to bring me closer. My breasts brushed his chest with every long, shivering breath I took.

"You are free now," whispered my husband at last, releasing me, "to do as you like. . . . How will you use your liberty?"

For an answer, I put my arms around his neck, sank back upon the pillows, pulling him down to me, and brought my wild mouth to his. . . .

Oregon Brown
by
Sara Orwig

Bestselling author of TIDES OF PASSION
and NEW ORLEANS

"The multi-faceted talent of Sara Orwig gleams as
bright as gold." —*Rave Reviews*

*With more than five million copies of her books in print,
Sara Orwig is without a doubt one of romance's top authors.
Her previous novels have been showered with praise and
awards, including five* Romantic Times *awards and numerous* Affaire de Coeur *awards.*

*Now Bantam Books is proud to present a new edition of one
of her most passionate novels—the story of a woman forced to
choose between fantasy and reality. . . .*

Charity Webster left the city for small-town Oklahoma
to assume the reins of the family company she had
inherited. With nothing behind her but a failed business and a shattered romance, and no one in her new
life except an aging aunt, Charity gives her nights to a
velvet-voiced late-night deejay . . . and to a fantasy
about the man behind the sexy, sultry voice.

But daylight brings her into head-on conflict with
another man, the wealthy O. O. Brown, who is maneu-
vering to acquire the family firm. Arrogant and all too
aware of his own charm, he still touches off a sensuous
spark in Charity that she can't deny . . . and she finds
herself torn between two men—one a mystery, the
other the keeper of her deepest secrets.

And don't miss these heart-stopping
romances from Bantam Books,
on sale in October:

OUTLAW by Susan Johnson

MOONLIGHT, MADNESS,
AND MAGIC
by Suzanne Forster,
Charlotte Hughes,
and Olivia Rupprecht

SATIN AND STEELE
by Fayrene Preston

And in hardcover from Doubleday:

SOMETHING BORROWED,
SOMETHING BLUE
by Gillian Karr

OFFICIAL RULES

To enter the sweepstakes below carefully follow all instructions found elsewhere in this offer.

The **Winners Classic** will award prizes with the following approximate maximum values: 1 Grand Prize: $26,500 (or $25,000 cash alternate); 1 First Prize: $3,000; 5 Second Prizes: $400 each; 35 Third Prizes: $100 each; 1,000 Fourth Prizes: $7.50 each. Total maximum retail value of Winners Classic Sweepstakes is $42,500. Some presentations of this sweepstakes may contain individual entry numbers corresponding to one or more of the aforementioned prize levels. To determine the Winners, individual entry numbers will first be compared with the winning numbers preselected by computer. For winning numbers not returned, prizes will be awarded in random drawings from among all eligible entries received. Prize choices may be offered at various levels. If a winner chooses an automobile prize, all license and registration fees, taxes, destination charges and, other expenses not offered herein are the responsibility of the winner. If a winner chooses a trip, travel must be complete within one year from the time the prize is awarded. Minors must be accompanied by an adult. Travel companion(s) must also sign release of liability. Trips are subject to space and departure availability. Certain black-out dates may apply.

The following applies to the sweepstakes named above:

No purchase necessary. You can also enter the sweepstakes by sending your name and address to: P.O. Box 508, Gibbstown, N.J. 08027. Mail each entry separately. Sweepstakes begins 6/1/93. Entries must be received by 12/30/94. Not responsible for lost, late, damaged, misdirected, illegible or postage due mail. Mechanically reproduced entries are not eligible. All entries become property of the sponsor and will not be returned.

Prize Selection/Validations: Selection of winners will be conducted no later than 5:00 PM on January 28, 1995, by an independent judging organization whose decisions are final. Random drawings will be held at 1211 Avenue of the Americas, New York, N.Y. 10036. Entrants need not be present to win. Odds of winning are determined by total number of entries received. Circulation of this sweepstakes is estimated not to exceed 200 million. All prizes are guaranteed to be awarded and delivered to winners. Winners will be notified by mail and may be required to complete an affidavit of eligibility and release of liability which must be returned within 14 days of date on notification or alternate winners will be selected in a random drawing. Any prize notification letter or any prize returned to a participating sponsor, Bantam Doubleday Dell Publishing Group, Inc., its participating divisions or subsidiaries, or the independent judging organization as undeliverable will be awarded to an alternate winner. Prizes are not transferable. No substitution for prizes except as offered or as may be necessary due to unavailability, in which case a prize of equal or greater value will be awarded. Prizes will be awarded approximately 90 days after the drawing. All taxes are the sole responsibility of the winners. Entry constitutes permission (except where prohibited by law) to use winners' names, hometowns, and likenesses for publicity purposes without further or other compensation. Prizes won by minors will be awarded in the name of parent or legal guardian.

Participation: Sweepstakes open to residents of the United States and Canada, except for the province of Quebec. Sweepstakes sponsored by Bantam Doubleday Dell Publishing Group, Inc., (BDD), 1540 Broadway, New York, NY 10036. Versions of this sweepstakes with different graphics and prize choices will be offered in conjunction with various solicitations or promotions by different subsidiaries and divisions of BDD. Where applicable, winners will have their choice of any prize offered at level won. Employees of BDD, its divisions, subsidiaries, advertising agencies, independent judging organization, and their immediate family members are not eligible.

Canadian residents, in order to win, must first correctly answer a time limited arithmetical skill testing question. Void in Puerto Rico, Quebec and wherever prohibited or restricted by law. Subject to all federal, state, local and provincial laws and regulations. For a list of major prize winners (available after 1/29/95): send a self-addressed, stamped envelope entirely separate from your entry to: Sweepstakes Winners, P.O. Box 517, Gibbstown, NJ 08027. Requests must be received by 12/30/94. DO NOT SEND ANY OTHER CORRESPONDENCE TO THIS P.O. BOX.

Don't miss these fabulous Bantam women's fiction titles Now on sale

• A WHISPER OF ROSES

by Teresa Medeiros, author of HEATHER AND VELVET

A tantalizing romance of love and treachery that sweeps from a medieval castle steeped in splendor to a crumbling Scottish fortress poised high above the sea. ____29408-3 $5.50/6.50 in Canada

• TENDER BETRAYAL

by Rosanne Bittner, author of OUTLAW HEARTS

The powerful tale of a Northern lawyer who falls in love with a beautiful plantation owner's daughter, yet willingly becomes the instrument of her family's destruction when war comes to the South. ____29808-9 $5.99/6.99 in Canada

• THE PAINTED LADY

by Lucia Grahame

"A unique and rare reading experience." —Romantic Times
In the bestselling tradition of Susan Johnson comes a stunningly sensual novel about sexual awakening set in 19th-century France and England. ____29864-X $4.99/5.99 in Canada

• OREGON BROWN

by Sara Orwig, author of NEW ORLEANS

*A classic passionate romance about a woman forced to choose between fantasy and reality.*____56088-3 $4.50/5.50 in Canada

Don't miss these fabulous Bantam women's fiction titles on sale in October

• OUTLAW

by Susan Johnson, author of SINFUL & FORBIDDEN

From the supremely talented mistress of erotic historical romance comes a sizzling love story of a fierce Scottish border lord who abducts his sworn enemy, a beautiful English woman — only to find himself a captive of her love.

___29955-7 $5.50/6.50 in Canada

• MOONLIGHT, MADNESS, AND MAGIC

by Suzanne Forster, Charlotte Hughes, and Olivia Rupprecht

Three romantic supernatural novellas set in 1785, 1872, and 1992. "Incredibly ingenious." — Romantic Times
"Something for everyone." — Gothic Journal
"An engaging read." — Publishers Weekly
"Exemplary." — Rendezvous   ___56052-2 $5.50/6.50 in Canada

• SATIN AND STEELE

by Fayrene Preston, co-author of THE DELANEY CHRISTMAS CAROL

Fayrene Preston's classic tale of a woman who thought she could never love again, and a man who thought love had passed him by.

___56457-9 $4.50/5.50 in Canada